FORTUNE
and the
GOLDEN
TROPHY

Stacy Gregg

HarperCollins *Children's Books*

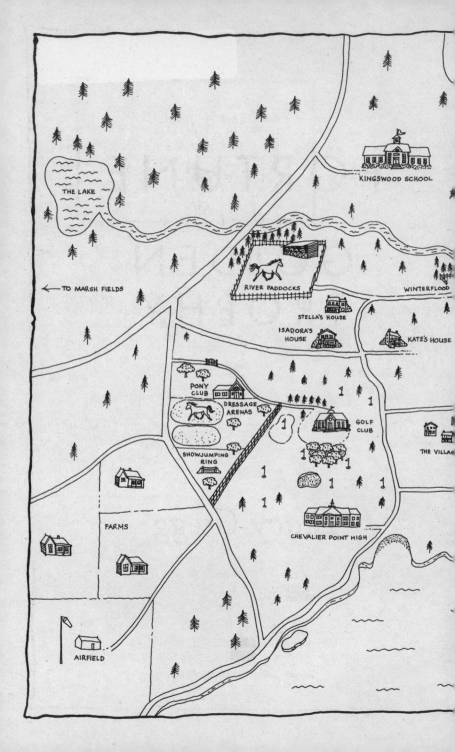

FORTUNE
and the
GOLDEN
TROPHY

CHEVALIER
POINT

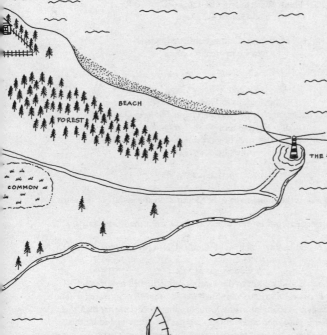

FOREST

BEACH

COMMON

THE POINT

GOAT ISLAND

For Gwen, who knows more about horses than I could hope
to learn in a lifetime. This book is dedicated to you for your
generosity and wisdom, and to the wonderful ponies that you
care for – Toddy, Hokey Pokey, Luka, Jasper and Migsy

www.stacygregg.co.uk

First published in Great Britain by HarperCollins *Children's Books* in 2009
This edition published in 2020
HarperCollins *Children's Books* is a division of HarperCollins*Publishers* Ltd,
HarperCollins Publishers
1 London Bridge Street
London SE1 9GF

HarperCollins*Publishers*
1st Floor, Watermarque Building, Ringsend Road
Dublin 4, Ireland

The HarperCollins website address is
www.harpercollins.co.uk
18

Text copyright © Stacy Gregg 2009
Illustrations © Fiona Land 2009
Cover design copyright © HarperCollins*Publishers* Ltd 2020
Cover photography © Shutterstock.com
CBBC logo © British Broadcasting Corporation 2016
All rights reserved.

ISBN 978–0–00–727032–3

Stacy Gregg asserts the moral right to be identified as the author of the work.

A CIP catalogue record for this title is available from the British Library.

Printed and bound in England by CPI Group (UK) Ltd, Croydon, CR0 4YY

MIX
Paper from
responsible sources
FSC™ C007454

This book is produced from independently certified FSC™ paper
to ensure responsible forest management.

For more information visit: www.harpercollins.co.uk/green

CHAPTER 1

The chestnut mare tensed up as the girth tightened around her belly. It had been a long time since she'd been ridden and she was excited by the weight of the saddle on her back. As she moved about nervously in the stall the girl with the long dark hair knew exactly how to handle her. She stayed calm, talking to her softly all the time as she cinched the straps up one more hole, before reaching for the bridle and gently slipping it over the mare's pretty, dished Arabian face.

"Easy, Blaze," said Issie Brown. She knew what the mare was thinking because she felt exactly the same way. It was so strange being in the stables at Winterflood Farm again, just the two of them, getting ready to ride. Issie could hardly believe that only a few days ago she had been in Spain, galloping across the sunburnt fields

7

of El Caballo Danza Magnifico. Now suddenly, here she was back in Chevalier Point. It felt so weird to be home.

The flight back from Madrid to New Zealand had been very long. Her mother had met her at the airport yesterday and Issie had collapsed into her mum's arms at the arrival gates, burying her face to hide her tears.

Mrs Brown couldn't understand why her daughter was so upset. What on earth had happened?

"It's Storm…" Issie had finally managed to gulp out.

"Storm?" Mrs Brown was even more confused. "But I got your email. You said he was safe. You told me you'd won him back in the race."

Issie took a deep breath and dried her eyes. "I did win him back. But he's still at El Caballo Danza Magnifico," she told her mother.

"For how long? Is Francoise organising his transport home?"

Issie shook her head. "No, Mum, you don't understand." She paused for a moment, unable to bring herself to say the words and acknowledge the awful truth. "Storm isn't coming home. He's going to stay in Spain. I've left him behind…"

The reality hit home when Issie arrived at Winterflood

Farm this morning and the colt wasn't there. The stables seemed so empty without Storm. The farm had been his home ever since he was born. Issie had been right there when his mother Blaze had given birth to him in these very stables. Over the past six months she had raised Storm, marvelling each day at the changes in him as he grew up from a baby foal to a strapping young colt. He wasn't just any foal – he was Blaze's son and he meant the world to Issie. She loved him so much. Letting him go had been the hardest thing she had ever done.

Roberto Nunez, owner of El Caballo Danza Magnifico, assured her that it wasn't forever. The colt would live at El Caballo Danza Magnifico until he was fully trained and then, one day, Issie would get him back again.

At least she still had Blaze. Issie ran her hand over the arch of the Anglo-Arab's elegant neck, smoothing down her flaxen mane. As Blaze turned her pretty face back towards her, Issie was struck once more by just how much the mare resembled her colt. Storm was a bay and Blaze was a chestnut, but mother and son still shared the same features, the dished nose, broad nostrils and wide, intelligent eyes that were the hallmarks of their Arabian bloodlines.

Blaze nickered softly, her dark eyes looking sorrowful as she nuzzled Issie. "You miss him, don't you, girl?" Issie said softly. "I know. Me too…"

A sudden noise in the corridor startled the mare and she pricked up her ears. There were footsteps outside the stall, and then the sound of a bolt sliding as the top of the Dutch door opened and there was Tom Avery smiling in at them. He was dressed in his favourite brown jersey and his mop of thick, dark, curly hair was held back by a tweed cheesecutter cap.

"I just came to check on you. Is everything all right?" he asked.

Issie nodded. "Blaze is fine, Tom. I haven't ridden her for over a year, or even seen her for the past month, so she's bound to be a little nervous about being saddled up again…"

"I wasn't talking about Blaze," Avery said, his voice heavy with concern. "I meant you, Issie. Are you OK?"

Avery knew only too well how painful it had been for Issie to leave Storm in Spain. Although she had tried to act all grown up about it, he knew that deep down she was heartbroken. He had tried to talk to her about it on the flight home, but Issie had been too upset. She had put on her earphones and blocked out the world the whole way back. Avery had the good sense to leave her alone. But now they were home, he could see that Issie was still miserable. When she arrived at the farm this morning she had hardly said a word to Avery, and her instructor couldn't help being worried about her.

Issie kept brushing Blaze and didn't look up. "I don't need you worrying about me too," she said defensively. "I've had Mum fussing over me ever since I got back. I was lucky she even let me out of her sight this morning."

"She's just concerned about you, Issie," said Avery gently. "It's understandable, after all you've been through…"

"I'm OK, Tom," Issie insisted unconvincingly. "I just wish I knew for sure… did I do the right thing?"

Avery nodded. "El Caballo Danza Magnifico is the best dressage school in the world. They'll give Storm the finest training. I have no doubt that leaving your colt behind was the right thing to do."

"So why does it hurt so much?" Issie asked, her voice trembling.

"It'll get better," said Avery gently. "I promise. And do you know what I always tell my riders to do when they're hurting?"

"What?"

"Get back on the horse." Avery smiled. "Of course, in

your case you're going to have to get back on two of them."

He was right. Even with Storm gone, Issie had her hands full. Blaze had recovered from having her foal and was ready to start serious training once more. Then there was Comet. The stocky skewbald had been Issie's star showjumper before she went away, and she was keen to get him primed for competition. The Chevalier Point Pony Club Annual General Meeting was being held tomorrow night, marking the beginning of a whole new season. Next weekend would be the first rally and then every weekend would be full of club days and competitions, dressage tests, one-day events and gymkhanas, and Issie had not one, but two super horses to ride!

Issie loved both her horses equally, but she was smart enough to know that they shouldn't be treated the same. While Blaze was a delicate purebred, Comet was the opposite – a rough customer like all of the Blackthorn Ponies. After running wild for years on her aunt's farmland, Blackthorns were a rugged breed, and they didn't need mollycoddling. So, for the past three weeks of winter rain, she had left Comet grazing down at the River Paddock where other pony-club horses grazed. She knew that the hardy little skewbald would be just fine to face the elements in his thick, waterproof New Zealand rug.

Blaze, on the other hand, was much more fragile. Her Anglo-Arabian bloodlines made her sensitive to the cold. So Avery had offered to keep the mare stabled at Winterflood Farm while they were away, and Stella and Kate, Issie's best friends, had promised to keep an eye on her.

Now Issie was home and the worst of the rain was over. Blaze would be fine at the River Paddock from now on and today Issie planned to hack the mare there. Blaze seemed to sense that they were about to leave the farm. She moved about restlessly, her metal horseshoes chiming on the concrete floor of the stable block as Issie walked her outside.

"Take it easy on her," Avery cautioned as he gave Issie a leg-up. "Blaze hasn't been ridden for a long time so she's bound to be a bit spooky."

He was right. As Issie rode down the long, poplar-lined driveway that led from Winterflood Farm Blaze seemed to take fright at every leaf that wobbled in the wind. When they reached the end of the drive and a pheasant flew up from the undergrowth beside them, Blaze startled and leapt forward as if she were about to bolt, but Issie held her back and calmed her down. She didn't panic at the mare's display of nerves and she never lost patience with her. Instead, she stayed relaxed in the saddle, whispering secret words to her pony in a soft, low voice, bonding with Blaze once more.

By the time they reached the wide grass verge of the riverbank that would take them to the River Paddock, Blaze wasn't spooking at all. She was still fresh though, and kept jogging, keen to break into a trot. Issie gave in and let the mare trot on, but Blaze still strained at the reins and Issie realised that the mare wouldn't be happy until she was let loose to gallop.

She also knew what Avery would say, that Blaze wasn't ready and they should take it slow, that galloping was a no-no. But at that moment Issie didn't care. She was desperate to blow the events of the past weeks away and escape from her own thoughts, if only for a moment. She needed to gallop just as much as her chestnut mare did.

Issie stood up in the stirrups, adjusted her weight into her heels and then gently let the reins slide through her fingers, inching them out slowly enough to give Blaze her head without losing control. She felt the mare rise up beneath her into a loping canter and then suddenly they were galloping, the grass below Blaze's hooves dissolving into a green blur as they sped on.

Issie could feel her pulse racing, the wind whipping against her face, cold air stinging her cheeks. It felt good. After the heartache of the past few days, being back on Blaze made her spirits soar. She was consumed by the rhythm of the horse beneath her, surging forward, leaving everything else behind.

Blaze was in full gallop now, her strides lengthening. Issie stayed low over the mare's neck and kept a tight hold on the reins. They were nearly at the River Paddock and she would need to slow the mare down soon, but not just yet.

As they came into view of the paddocks Issie found that she actually had to work quite hard to bring Blaze down from a gallop. The mare was bristling with energy and high spirits and didn't want to stop. But Issie worked the bit in her mouth and slowly Blaze gave in to her rider and began to canter and then, reluctantly, to trot.

Issie posted up and down in the saddle in a brisk rising trot, her eyes scanning the paddocks ahead of her. She was looking for Comet, but she was also trying to see if she could spot the other horses too. Kate and Stella both grazed their horses here at the River Paddock. Toby, Kate's horse, was a rangy, bay Thoroughbred gelding, while Stella rode a cheeky, chocolate-coloured mare named Coco.

In the shade of the willow trees down near the river, Issie caught sight of Comet. He was grazing happily next to Toby, but there was no sign of Coco. Issie's eyes swept the paddock. She couldn't see her anywhere.

Coco was probably hidden out of sight. There were lots of trees and dips and hollows in the River Paddock where a horse might be concealed. The mare was bound to be here somewhere.

Then Issie caught a glimpse of something and suddenly she wasn't so calm about Coco any more. At the far end of the paddock, beyond the willow trees near the river, there was something huge lying down on the ground. At a distance, it looked to Issie like the shape of a horse – and it wasn't moving. Issie felt a sudden surge of panic. It had to be Coco!

There are lots of perfectly normal reasons why a horse might be lying down. But alarm bells were ringing in Issie's brain. The horse lying there looked odd. Something was definitely wrong. Issie's first thought was colic, and it filled her with dread. Coco was a greedy little pony and with the new spring grass coming through she could easily have eaten too much and become colicky. That would explain why she was lying down. But lying down was the worst thing a pony with colic might do. Stomach pains could make Coco kick at her own tummy with her hooves and she might injure herself horribly. If she did have colic, Issie needed to get her up immediately. She had to get Coco walking and keep her moving until she could fetch the vet.

By the time she reached the gates of the paddock, Issie was in a blind panic. She pulled Blaze up and vaulted off, hunting desperately in her pockets for the padlock key. Eventually, she managed to find it and work the lock. She pushed the gate open and led Blaze through.

Toby and Comet, both excited to see another horse at the paddock, did the normal thing and trotted up straight away to greet Blaze. The horse on the ground, on the other hand, didn't budge. It was lying there at the end of the paddock, utterly still. Now Issie really feared the worst. Was the mare even alive?

Slamming the gate shut behind her, Issie stuck her foot in the stirrup and bounced back up into the saddle. She urged Blaze straight into a canter and clucked the mare on through the paddock towards the dark shape on the ground.

The horse was still lying there, perfectly motionless. However, as they came closer, Issie began to have doubts. Was it really Coco? It was quite definitely a horse – Issie could see the outline of its fat belly and legs sticking out from beneath a winter paddock rug. But as she approached, she noticed that it didn't actually look like Coco. It was too big for starters. Also, getting even nearer, Issie could see that the horse wasn't chocolate brown either. It was a piebald, with black and white patches, a bit like a magpie.

There was no time to feel relieved though. Whoever this horse might be, it was still in big trouble.

As Blaze reached its side, Issie had been hoping for some sign that the animal was still alive. Surely a healthy horse would raise its head to acknowledge them? But this horse didn't even twitch a muscle as Issie dismounted and began to walk towards it.

Issie was just a few metres away from the piebald when she heard the noise. She had never heard anything like it before. It sounded like a troll grunting. Not that she had ever heard a troll grunt obviously, but it was that sort of sound, deep and guttural – almost otherworldly.

Issie took a few tentative steps forward. She was right up close to the piebald and there was no doubt that the noise was indeed coming from the horse. Now that she was right next to it, Issie could see the winter rug that covered the horse's stomach rising and falling in time to the noise. Issie stared at the piebald lying on the ground in utter disbelief. This horse wasn't sick or dead. It was fast asleep – and it was snoring.

Issie was about to take another step forward when the black and white horse suddenly stopped making the troll grunts and raised its head off the ground. Yep, there was no doubt about it. The piebald had been asleep all right!

Issie didn't know whether to feel angry or relieved as she watched the pony lumber to its feet in a rather ungainly fashion. The gelding shook out his mane and looked at her with a dopey, heavy-lidded expression on his face.

Issie stared as the piebald began to graze just a few metres in front of her. He was about the same size as Blaze, maybe fourteen-two hands. It was hard to be sure though because he wasn't shaped like Blaze in the slightest. He was a tubby pony. Clearly, the only thing he really liked as much as sleeping was eating. He was a true piebald, covered in big black and white splodges, with chunky white streaks through his black mane. He had a white muzzle and a star on his forehead which radiated out so that his whole face was sprinkled with white hairs in a salt-and-pepper effect.

It was a bit of an ugly face, Issie assessed clinically, slightly too large and out of proportion with his body, and with a Roman nose to boot. As far as Issie could tell with his rug on, the pony seemed to have decent enough conformation, apart from being overweight, but he was certainly no oil painting.

Even now that he was awake the piebald didn't seem particularly alert. He cast a vacant glance at Blaze, showing a complete lack of interest in the mare. He displayed even less interest in Issie who was still standing there, slack-jawed and staring at him. The piebald gave what looked like a yawn, then turned his rump on them both, lowered his head and ambled off.

Issie was gobsmacked. She had never seen anything like it. Horses hardly ever lay down to sleep. They certainly didn't snore. And she'd never met a horse who wasn't in the least bit curious to meet another new horse before.

"Well, I'm just glad you're OK," Issie said. She was talking to herself though because the piebald wasn't listening. He was grazing away and resolutely ignoring her. "You are one kooky little piebald." Issie shook her head. "Whoever owns you has got their hands full."

She didn't realise how right she was.

CHAPTER 2

Issie poked about in the tack shed, hoping to find some clue as to who owned the piebald in the paddock, but he remained a mystery. However, there was a saddle that looked about the right size for him and a bridle too. She also noticed that Coco's tack was missing. It was possible that Stella had taken it home to clean, but that was unlikely. Stella hardly *ever* cleaned her tack and was frequently being told off by Tom Avery for having sloppy turn-out on rally days.

Issie hung up Blaze's bridle and put the mare's saddle and numnah on top of a sawhorse. Then she headed for the back corner of the shed. Next to a big pile of winter rugs, right where she had left it, was her bike. She wheeled it out with Blaze's rug over the handlebars, then put the rug on her pony, gave her a carrot and slipped her halter off. Blaze trotted over to join Comet and Toby. There were a few snorts and ears back before the three of them remembered that they were best friends and trotted away happily together.

The piebald, meanwhile, was lying down and snoring once more. Issie shook her head in amazement, wheeled her bike out to the road, padlocked the gates behind her and set off for home.

Issie hoped that her mother would be there when she got back. She was desperate to tell someone about the mysterious arrival of the strange pony in the paddock.

"Mum?" Issie called as she shucked off her riding boots at the front door. "I'm back! Are you home?"

"We're in here!" Mrs Brown called back. "In the kitchen."

We're in here? What did that mean? Who was there?

Issie walked down the hall to the kitchen. Mrs Brown was at the kitchen worktop, pouring hot water from the kettle into the teapot. Standing beside her, putting some chocolate biscuits on a plate, was a boy who looked a couple of years older than Issie. He had black hair and his fringe, which was far too long, fell over his face as he turned around. He pushed the fringe back carelessly with his hand revealing a pair of penetrating blue eyes. He looked almost unbearably handsome and Issie felt her heart leap. The last time she had seen this boy he had been kissing her goodbye on the front lawn of Blackthorn Farm.

"Aidan!" Issie couldn't believe it. "Ohmygod!"

There was no chance of kissing Aidan now, even if he was supposed to officially be her boyfriend, because her mum was standing there staring at them both. And besides, even if her mum hadn't been there, Issie thought, Aidan was acting kind of odd. She would have expected him to come up and at least give her a hug, but he was being all cool, sort of distant and aloof.

"So," he said, hiding his eyes under his fringe, acting casual in a really awkward way, "how have you been? How was the trip back from Spain?"

"Good," said Issie, suddenly feeling uncomfortable. "I sent you a postcard. Didn't you get it?"

"Yeah," Aidan said, "I got it. Why didn't you call me? I thought you'd call me when you got back…"

"I was going to," Issie said, "but I've only been back for, like, a day."

"Sure," Aidan said, "you've been busy. I understand…" But he didn't look like he understood at all; in fact, he looked rather put out.

"What are you doing here anyway?" asked Issie.

Mrs Brown put down the teapot and placed her hands on her hips. "See? I told you!" she said to Aidan. "Issie had no idea you were coming either. Oh, this is so typical of Hester!"

Issie didn't understand. "What are you talking about, Mum?"

Mrs Brown shook her head. "It appears that your Aunt Hester had another one of her genius plans that she forgot to tell us about. She's sent poor Aidan here out of the blue. He was just explaining it to me when you arrived."

"Aidan?" Issie was still confused. "What's going on?"

"Ummm," Aidan began, "there seems to have been a bit of a miscommunication. I thought you and your mum were expecting me. Didn't you get the email that Hester sent you?"

Issie shook her head. "I only got back from Spain yesterday. I haven't checked my emails for days."

"Oh," Aidan said, "so I guess you got a bit of a shock finding the piebald at the River Paddock?"

"Totally!" Issie said. "How did you know? I turn up at the paddock, Coco is missing and instead there's this crazy piebald lying on the ground fast asleep, snoring like a train."

"I don't have a clue about the Coco part," Aidan said, "but I can explain the piebald. I drove him up from Blackthorn Farm in the horse truck this morning and dropped him off at the paddock."

"But why is he in the River Paddock?" Issie was still confused. "Who does he belong to?"

Aidan groaned. "That's the thing... Hester was supposed to tell you... I thought you already knew." He paused. "Issie, I don't know how to say this, but..." Aidan winced, "he's yours. I brought him here for you."

By the time Issie was on to her third chocolate biscuit, she had managed to make sense of Aidan's explanation.

It appeared that Issie's lovely but utterly mad Aunty Hester was in trouble yet again. The last time Issie had visited Blackthorn Farm, a rambling old country manor high up in the hills near Gisborne, she had been helping Hester out of a tight spot. Her aunt ran the Daredevil Ponies, a troupe of stunt horses who were the best in the movie business. When film work had suddenly dried up earlier in the year Hester hit hard times and was on the brink of selling Blackthorn Farm and her menagerie of four-legged movie stars.

Luckily for Hester, Issie and Aidan, her farm manager, had come to the rescue. They both entered the Horse of the Year Show – Issie on Comet and Aidan on Destiny – and between them they won enough prize money to help Hester save the farm. Hester had been so grateful she had made the two of them her business partners.

It turned out that Comet had put in such a superstar performance at the Horse of the Year that Hester's ponies subsequently became hot property on the showjumping circuit. Every showjumping rider in the country wanted a Blackthorn Pony in their stable and they were prepared to pay big money for them. Hester and Aidan suddenly found themselves with a lucrative business on their hands, schooling up and selling Blackthorn Ponies.

"Hester and I have been really busy training half a dozen up-and-coming young jumpers," Aidan told Issie. "We'd planned to sell them at the end of the season. Everything was going really well until that movie, the same one that was cancelled earlier in the year, suddenly sprang back to life. Now it's all on again and filming starts in two weeks."

"I know. You emailed me about it in Spain. But that's brilliant news, isn't it?" Issie asked.

"Yes – and no," said Aidan. "Hester has been working like crazy behind the scenes, trying to get the stunt horses ready in time for the cameras. She doesn't have any time right now for the farm and it will only get worse when filming begins. I've been left behind to look after the Blackthorn Ponies. Some of them are at a crucial stage in their schooling, plus I'm snowed under with farm work. I was beginning to panic that I wouldn't be able to cope, and that was when Hester decided we needed to involve you."

"Me?" Issie squeaked nervously.

"Yeah, well, you are a partner in the business." Aidan smiled. "So Hester had the idea of bringing a few of the young horses up to Chevalier Point for training."

"A few? You mean there's more of them?" squeaked Issie again.

"Uh-huh. I brought three of them with me in the horse truck. You've met the piebald. The other two are a chestnut and a dark brown – Jasper and Marmite. Both of them need loads of work too."

Aidan grinned at the look of horror on Issie's face. "Don't worry. I'm not going to ask you to look after them as well. You'll have your hands full with the piebald. I've asked Tom if he'll take care of the other two. I've just taken them to Winterflood Farm."

"Is that where your horse truck is?" Issie realised that she hadn't seen it parked outside when she arrived.

"Uh-huh. I'm going back there shortly to help him settle them in, but I thought I'd better come here and see you first to explain about the piebald."

"What's up with that pony? He's totally kooky," Issie said.

"He's a Blackthorn Pony, born and bred," Aidan said. "So I figure he's got a huge jump buried in him somewhere, but I really haven't had the chance to do any schooling on him yet. He's been broken in, but apart from that he's just been turned out for two seasons now. I've only ridden him a few times in the past six months. I got on him for the first time in ages last week. I thought I'd better try him before bringing him here. Anyway, I thought he'd be all fizzy after not being ridden for so long, but he just about fell asleep under me. The only thing he loves, as far as I can tell, is sleeping."

"I noticed!" Issie said.

"He's kinda… quirky," continued Aidan, "but he's got no vices. He doesn't buck or rear or anything, he's just, well... you'll see... he's a bit of a... character. He needs someone like you, Issie. Someone who can focus on him and bring out the best."

"But I already have Blaze and Comet! How can I focus on him when I have two other horses I'm supposed to be riding?" Issie protested.

"I'm working six horses a day at the moment," Aidan pointed out. "I'm only asking you to manage with three."

"Yes, but that's your job!" Issie objected. "I've got school to worry about."

"Well, that's good to hear," Mrs Brown said wryly as she reached between Issie and Aidan to restock the chocolate biscuit plate. "I've never noticed you being particularly concerned about your horses getting in the way of school work before, Isadora. You *have* grown up since you got back from Spain!"

Her mother's sarcasm was not lost on her, but Issie decided to ignore it. "I've got exams this term," she continued. "It's different. And looking after three horses is a lot harder than two."

Aidan's smile faded. "Issie, I wouldn't be asking you to do this unless it was important. Hester has only just got the farm back on its feet again. You and I are her business partners now and she needs us to pitch in. Maybe by next season, when things have improved, she can hire another stable hand to help out with the training, but until then she's relying on you."

Aidan brushed his dark fringe back and looked into Issie's eyes. She remembered the last time he had stared at her like that. It was just before his lips had touched hers, on the lawn under the cherry trees.

She remembered feeling as if her knees were going to buckle beneath her as she stood there that day. Now, when Aidan smiled at her, she felt herself going weak all over again. "Come on, Issie, what do you say? It's just one horse. How much trouble can he be?"

Issie sighed. Aidan made it impossible to say no. Still, she had a feeling she was going to regret this.

"What exactly does Hester want me to do with him?"

"Compete on him," said Aidan. "Right now that piebald isn't worth a lot because he doesn't have enough experience. But if you could ride him for the next few months and win a few ribbons or maybe even some trophies with him on the gymkhana circuit then he'd be worth a whole lot more."

"You want me to take him on the show circuit and win championship ribbons?" Issie was stunned. "Aidan! Have you *seen* the state of him?"

Aidan gave her a cheeky grin. "What's the matter, Issie? Are you saying that you're only a good rider if you've got a fancy horse like Blaze underneath you to rely on? If the piebald is too tough for you to handle..."

"I didn't mean that!" Issie cut him off. "All right," she sighed, "I'll do my best with him, but you've seen what he's like – I'm not a miracle worker! I'll try, but tell Aunty Hess that I'm not making her any promises."

"Great!" Aidan said with obvious relief. Then he looked at his watch. "Listen, I hate to do this, but I have to go. I promised Tom I would help with the horses. And after that I need to head straight back to Blackthorn Farm."

Issie's heart sank. "Really? You can't stay?"

Aidan shook his head. "No. I'm only here for the day. I can't leave the horses and the other animals at Blackthorn overnight without anyone there to feed and check on them. I'll try and make it back through soon though – maybe next week?"

"OK," Issie said with an air of resignation. She had dreamt about seeing Aidan so often over the past month, but those dreams definitely didn't involve him turning up with a nutty piebald pony to dump on her before racing off again.

As Aidan grabbed Avery's car keys and headed for the door Issie walked with him. She was beginning to think Aidan was going to leave without giving her a kiss goodbye, but then at the last minute he leaned over and gave her a hasty peck on the cheek. The cheek! What sort of kiss was that? Aidan, meanwhile, was looking decidedly uncomfortable again. Something was definitely up.

"Is anything wrong?" asked Issie nervously.

"Yeah, well, I had something I wanted to say to you…" Aidan said.

"What is it?" Issie felt her pulse quickening. What was going on? Was he trying to break up with her? Was that it?

They stood there for a moment on the front step, both of them afraid to speak. And then, just as Aidan was about to open his mouth, Mrs Brown appeared beside them.

"You forgot your coat," she said, handing Aidan a navy puffa jacket.

He froze with embarrassment, being caught in an awkward moment by Issie's mum. "Thanks," he mumbled, taking the jacket. Then he looked at Issie. "Anyway, I'll talk to you later, OK?" he said. "I'll give you a call." And with that, he headed off down the front steps towards the gate.

Aidan was just opening the gate when Issie suddenly realised she'd forgotten to ask him a very important question.

"The piebald!" she called out after him. "What's his name?"

Aidan turned to look at her. "I was hoping you wouldn't ask that," he said. "I've had no luck coming up with anything so far. I'm stuck, I'm afraid. I thought I'd leave it up to you."

"How about Snoozy?" Issie suggested sarcastically.

"Up to you," Aidan said. "He's your horse for now." He looked at his watch. "Oh, man, I've gotta go. Avery will be waiting!" He looked intently at Issie. "I'll call you, OK? Good luck with the piebald."

"Yeah, thanks," Issie muttered under her breath as Aidan waved goodbye. "Thanks a whole bunch…"

CHAPTER 3

The Coco mystery was solved not long after Aidan departed when there was a knock at the door.

"That'll be Stella," Mrs Brown said. "I told her you'd be home shortly. She said she was coming over as soon as you were back."

When Issie opened the door Stella leapt through it and smothered her friend in a mammoth hug.

"You're back!" she squealed. "Ohmygod! I missed you so much. Heaps of stuff has happened and it's been awful not having you here…"

"I just went down to the River Paddock," Issie interrupted her. "Where's Coco?"

"That's what I mean about it being awful," Stella said. Her expression was grim beneath her red curly hair. "Coco is gone."

"Gone? Where? What do you mean?"

"I sold her."

"What?" Issie was stunned. "When? Why didn't you tell me?"

"Last week. I didn't tell you because you weren't here obviously," Stella said glumly. "I was getting so big on her – I had to sell her really. Remember how you said my feet were almost dragging on the ground?"

"Did you have to do it while I was away?" said Issie. "I didn't even get the chance to say goodbye to her!"

"I know, I'm sorry," Stella said, "but they wanted to take her immediately."

She looked really miserable. "I wish you'd been here when she left. It was so awful watching them load her on the horse float and drive away. I've been crying all week."

"Who bought her?" Issie asked.

"Do you remember Kitty from the riding school at Blackthorn Farm?" Stella sniffed. "Well, her mum said she could finally have her own pony and so they came and tried Coco out, and Kitty totally fell in love with her."

"Stella, that's great!" said Issie. "Kitty is super-nice and she's a really good rider."

Stella didn't seem at all cheered up by this. The idea

of her precious Coco being ridden by anyone else, even Kitty, didn't make her any happier. "She's all right I suppose," she agreed grudgingly.

"But what about pony club?" Issie pointed out. "The new season is just about to start. It's only a week until our first rally. What will you do?"

"That's my big news!" Stella perked up. "He arrives tomorrow, so I'll have him in time for the first rally next weekend."

"Who arrives tomorrow?" Issie was confused.

"My new horse!"

"You've got a new horse already?"

"Well, not exactly," Stella admitted. "He's just on trial. I had one ride on him to try him out and now they've let me take him for a week to see if we get on. His name is Misty and he's a fleabitten grey."

"Has Tom checked him over yet?"

Stella shook her head. "He said he'd have a look at him for me this week before the first rally day."

"I can't believe it's the beginning of the season already!" Issie said. "I wish I only had one horse. Now I'm stuck with three of them at once."

Stella rolled her eyes. "Issie! Just listen to yourself! Complaining because you have too many horses?

Most riders would kill to have just one pony and you're lucky enough to have three."

"I know," Issie checked herself. "I mean it's amazing having three horses, but honestly, how will I cope? I was really looking forward to riding Blaze and Comet this season and now this great piebald lump from Blackthorn Farm has turned up and I have to train him too…"

"So Aidan just dropped him off and left him with you?" Stella said.

"Pretty much." Issie nodded. She was still thinking about how odd Aidan had been when he'd turned up. Had he been trying to break up with her? If he was, she didn't feel ready to tell Stella about it. Not yet anyway.

"What's the piebald like?" Stella asked.

"He's really tubby with a bit of a Roman nose and he's got big black and white patches."

"Does he have a name?"

Issie shook her head. "Aidan says I have to name him."

"That is so cool!" Stella grinned. "I've always wanted to name my own horse."

"What do you think I should call him then?"

"How about Tonto?" Stella said. "You know, like the Lone Ranger because he's a cowboy colour?"

"What about Patchy?" Issie suggested.

"You're kidding, right?" Stella pulled a face. "I tell you what, why don't you come over to my house with Kate tomorrow night before the AGM. We can order a pizza and come up with pony names together."

"OK," Issie agreed.

"It must be awful for the poor piebald," said Stella. "Imagine not knowing what you're called! No wonder he's a bit odd. I'm sure you'll get on better once you've named him."

Issie hoped Stella was right. Maybe her feelings about the new horse would change once he had a name, but right now the only thing she could think of calling him was a big fat nuisance.

From the very start, the following night was a disaster. First of all, the pizza arrived late and the girls were grossed out when they took a bite and discovered it had anchovies on it. Then the pony-naming session wasn't a great success either. Stella and Kate's list of suggestions all sounded like cuddly toys.

"I am not calling my horse Mr Snuggles!" Issie finally snapped.

"Geez, OK!" said Kate. "There's no need to get grumpy."

It was at that point that Stella's mum, Mrs Tarrant, put her head round the bedroom door. "The AGM begins in ten minutes," she said. "Pile into the car and let's go!"

By the time Mrs Tarrant and the girls arrived at the Chevalier Point clubroom, most of the rows of fold-out chairs were already filled up with club members and their parents. There were loads of other riders that the girls hadn't seen since last season and the first person that they bumped into was Morgan Chatswood-Smith.

"You're back!" Issie said, giving Morgan a huge hug.

"How was the showjumping circuit?" asked Stella.

Morgan's mum, Araminta, was a professional showjumper, and for the past season she had taken Morgan on the road with her, touring the country with her string of showjumping horses.

"Pretty cool," Morgan said, "but you have to work really hard. I was doing loads of grooming for the other riders and I hardly ever got to do any riding myself."

"At least you didn't have to go to school! I would kill for three whole months without school work," Stella said.

Morgan shook her head, "I wish! I still had to do the work – Mum home-schooled me. And you know how tough she can be about horse riding? Well, she's even worse with maths!"

The girls nodded knowingly at this. When Issie first met Morgan she had been envious of her having such a famous horse-riding mum. But when Araminta put too much pressure on her daughter to compete Morgan started acting strangely – even sabotaging the other riders' equipment at the pony club! Issie had found out what was going on and confronted Morgan and Araminta with the truth. Since then, things had been much better between them. Even so, Issie could tell that Morgan still struggled to live up to the high expectations of her competitive mother.

"Why don't you guys come and sit with us?" Morgan said to Issie. "We've saved you seats."

Issie looked across the clubroom and spotted Araminta in a seat in the front row next to Tom Avery. Two other riders, Dan Halliday and Ben MacIntosh, were sitting next to them.

Dan smiled and waved when he saw the girls. Issie grinned and waved back. It was hard to believe that there had been so much drama with Dan just a few months ago. He used to have a crush on Issie and there had been a stand-off between him and Aidan at the Horse of the Year Show as they fought for her attention. But that was all over now. Dan and Issie were back to being just the way they were before – really good friends.

"Hey, Issie!" Dan called down the row to her as the four girls took their seats. "What's this I hear about you having a new horse? What's he like?"

"Don't ask!" Issie groaned. Everyone had taken their seats now and the meeting was about to begin. Issie glanced anxiously over her shoulder.

"What's wrong?" Kate asked.

"Natasha Tucker's not here," Issie said. She scanned the room again to be sure, but there was no sign of the sour-faced girl with the stiff blonde plaits. Issie couldn't help but feel relieved.

"You want to know my theory about Stuck-up Tucker?" Stella said to Issie. "I think she has a love-hate relationship with you."

"You're wrong," Issie sighed. "There's definitely no love. She can't stand me."

Any hope that Issie had of ever being friends with Natasha had disappeared forever after the Horse of the Year Show. Bratty Natasha had been training on her horse Fabergé with her expensive private trainer Ginty McLintoch and she totally expected to win. No wonder then that she was furious when Issie and Comet beat her in the big competition that day.

It made matters even worse, when Natasha and Ginty McLintoch offered to buy Comet after the show, and Issie refused to sell him to them. Ever since then, it had officially been war between the two riders.

The meeting had been scheduled for 8 p.m. and at ten past, Mrs Tarrant stepped up to the podium. She tapped the microphone to make sure it was working and then began to read from the stack of papers in front of her.

"As your departing club president, I am going to take you through the minutes of our last meeting…"

"Ohmygod," Stella hissed to Issie. "I'm bored already!"

Issie couldn't help giggling, but she quickly pulled herself together again as Avery shot the girls a stern glance.

Stella was right though; it was hard not to fidget as Mrs Tarrant went on about club fees and equipment rosters. Finally, after what seemed like hours, she plonked her stack of papers back down on the podium in front of her. "That takes care of all our business from last season."

"Crikey! About time!" Stella muttered. The girls tried hard to suppress their giggles again.

"As you know, we've already voted in the new

committee for the year and tonight I'll be 'handing over the reins'!" Mrs Tarrant grinned at her own joke, which she thought was very funny since this was a pony club, but no one else seemed to get it.

"Anyway, at this stage in the evening, I was hoping to hand you over to our new club president, Oliver Tucker... but I don't think he's arrived yet..."

At that exact moment, as if on cue, the front door of the clubroom swung open.

"Ahhh, Mr Tucker," Mrs Tarrant said. "I had just about given up on you."

"That's our new club president." Dan leant across to Issie. "Natasha Tucker's dad."

"Really?" Issie said, staring at the tall, blond man in the suit who now had everyone in the room turning around to look at him. "I've never, ever seen him here before."

It wasn't surprising that Issie had never seen Oliver Tucker before because, despite the fact that he had spent a fortune on Natasha's ponies, until tonight he had never set foot on the grounds of the Chevalier Point Pony Club. He was a big-shot businessman, far too busy with corporate takeovers and property deals to make time for his daughter's little hobbies.

Oliver Tucker wore a designer suit that stretched taut over his pot belly, well-padded from extravagant company lunches. *My friends call me Ollie,* he would often say by way of introduction. But this was untrue. No one called him "Ollie" because Oliver Tucker had no friends. He didn't care – money was much more important and he had loads of that. This was just as well because he'd spent a fair chunk of it on horses to keep his daughter happy.

"I can't believe he's the new pony-club president," whispered Issie.

"Mum says he won the ballot because no one else dared to stand against him," Dan shrugged.

"Ohhh, scary!" Stella said. "So if that's Natasha's dad, then where is Natasha?"

Stella's question was answered by a grunting noise on the stairs right behind Mr Tucker. "Hey, Dad! Urghh!… Can I get a little help here?"

Natasha Tucker appeared in the doorway behind her dad. She wore her trademark scowl and seemed to be struggling to carry something enormous in her arms.

"Hurry up, Dad!" Natasha squealed. "Take an end. I'm going to drop it!"

There was a definite flicker of impatience on Mr

Tucker's face as he came to his daughter's aid and took one end of the object, helping to ease it in through the door.

The mystery object, shrouded in a velvet curtain, was about a metre wide and almost as tall as Natasha. Whatever it was, clearly it was very heavy as it took both Natasha and Mr Tucker to carry it through the clubroom towards the podium.

"Careful, Natasha, careful!" Mr Tucker instructed as they manoeuvred their way between the rows of chairs to the front of the room. "Hang on to it! OK, now take a step to the left… no! My left, Natasha! Not yours! For Pete's sake, can't you do anything right?"

Natasha's face was puce beneath her blonde plaits as she dropped her end of the object with a thud on to the floor. Mr Tucker tutted at her and lowered his end gently so that the mystery object stood in front of the audience, next to the podium.

"Good evening!" Mr Tucker said, greeting them all. "As Mrs Tarrant said, I'm your new club president. I'd just like to say that this is a great moment for the Chevalier Point Pony Club. It isn't every day that a man like myself, with formidable business expertise, makes himself available for such a role…"

Mr Tucker had been expecting applause at this point and was clearly disappointed when he was met with stunned silence. Unabashed, he continued. "As your new president I have many great plans for this pony club, which you will hear in good time. Tonight, however, I thought this would be the perfect occasion to announce some very big news for the senior riders in the room.

"Many of you have enjoyed the pleasure of Natasha's company here at the pony club over the years." Mr Tucker gestured to his daughter, who had found a seat across the aisle from Issie and was watching her dad speak with a smug expression on her face.

"It seemed only fitting that the Tucker family should donate a special trophy in Natasha's honour to commemorate her great achievements at the Chevalier Point Pony Club."

Stella, who couldn't believe what she was hearing, suddenly doubled over and began to have a coughing fit.

Mr Tucker frowned at the interruption and continued. "The Tucker family believe in rewarding success. Most of you will never achieve as much as my daughter has with the calibre of horses I've bought her, but it never hurts to dream, eh?"

There were astonished mumbles from the audience at

the rudeness of this remark, but Mr Tucker never noticed when he was being rude and ploughed on. "Underneath this curtain is my contribution to the Chevalier Point Pony Club – a grand prize that will be awarded each year to the senior rider who accumulates the most points in the Open Gymkhana, which will be held at the end of next month, here at the club."

He stretched out a hand, gripped the corner of the velvet cloth and gave it a firm yank. The velvet fell away dramatically as the trophy was revealed.

"Ohmygod!" Stella gasped. The trophy looked like it had come from a popstar millionaire's mansion. It was a rearing horse over a metre high, coated from hoof to head in brilliant gold. The horse's eyes were made of turquoise, its mane sparkled with diamanté crystals and its hooves were studded with fake rubies. The giant gold statue was set on an ornate walnut veneer base, upon which, in grandiose, curlicued gilt letters, were the words: *Natasha Tucker Memorial Trophy*.

"Memorial? I thought you had to be dead to have a memorial named after you?" Kate hissed.

"That's a trophy? It looks like an explosion in a jewellery shop," Stella giggled. Issie, however, wasn't laughing quite so hard. She was in a state of shock.

Where did Stuck-up Tucker get the nerve?

"I can't believe she named a trophy after *herself*!" Issie whispered. "Don't you have to, like, win Badminton or the Olympics or something before you can do that?"

As Mr Tucker stood there expectantly Mrs Tarrant tried to lead a round of rather reluctant applause. This soon petered out and nobody seemed to know what to do next. Finally, Natasha stood up and whispered something to her father.

Mr Tucker nodded and then cleared his throat. "My daughter just wants to make it clear that, of course, as a senior rider herself at Chevalier Point this year, she is also eligible to compete alongside the other riders for the Tucker Trophy."

"You are kidding me!" Stella squeaked. "She's competing to win her own trophy?"

Issie was stunned. Only Natasha Tucker could possibly have come up with something so outrageous!

Standing next to her father at the podium, Natasha looked over at Issie, Stella and Kate, who were sitting with their jaws hanging open, and gave them a self-satisfied smirk.

As she walked back out of the clubroom behind her father she paused for a moment and looked Issie straight in the eyes. "You should go up and get a close look at the trophy while you can. Daddy's leaving it here in the clubroom on display for the next two months, until the gymkhana, so you'll get the chance to see it." Then she added with a sneer, "After that, it'll be going home with me – Daddy's already built a display case for it in the living room."

"Don't you think you should actually wait until you win it first before you build a case for it, Natasha?" Issie replied. "There are a lot of good senior riders at Chevalier Point you know…"

"And you think you're the best, don't you?" sneered Natasha. "You always have done. You act like you're better than me. Well, OK then, here's your chance to prove it!"

"I wasn't saying…" Issie began, but Natasha cut her off.

"You're not the best rider at this pony club, Isadora. In fact, you're not even in my league any more. I've got a better horse and a better instructor than you and I plan to show everyone when I take home that trophy at the end of the gymkhana!"

And with that, the bratty blonde turned on her heels and swept out of the clubroom, leaving Issie sitting there, gobsmacked.

Issie had known that there was no love lost between her and Natasha, but she hadn't been prepared for this latest outburst. She had no idea how much Natasha seemed to genuinely loathe her!

Natasha had Issie in her sights and their rivalry was about to come to a head in the battle for this trophy. The new season at Chevalier Point had begun and they were off to a cracking start.

CHAPTER 4

Stella was so excited about the arrival of Misty that she convinced Mrs Tarrant to get her off school early on Wednesday so that she could meet the pony when he arrived. By the time Issie and Kate had changed out of their school uniforms and cycled down to the River Paddock, Stella was unloading the fleabitten grey from the horse float, beaming with pride over her new pony. Her happiness was shattered just a few moments later when Avery turned up, took one look at Misty and announced that the trial was over.

"I'm sorry, but Misty is going straight home again," he told Stella bluntly.

"But why?" Stella said. "He's only just got here. You haven't even seen me ride him!"

"I don't need to, Stella." Avery said. "Look at this pony's conformation! He has a ewe neck, cow hocks and a parrot mouth!"

Stella boggled at this. "You mean he's part-sheep, part-cow and part-parrot? *I* thought he was a pony!"

Avery shook his head. "Don't be daft. They're common horse terms for conformation problems. You see how this pony's neck has no muscle on the top? That's a ewe neck. And look how his hocks point inwards and his back legs splay apart at the ground. That's cow hocks – and it can cause permanent lameness. You can see the parrot mouth too – the way his top lip sticks out over the bottom one like a parrot's beak. It means he'll have real problems with his teeth."

"He looks OK to me," Stella protested. She wasn't about to let Misty go without a fight.

Avery sighed. "Maybe if he just had one fault, or even a couple of conformation problems, I would still let you trial him. But this horse is like a handbook on what not to buy."

He looked at Stella. "These are serious faults, Stella. As your instructor I can't possibly recommend that you trial him. I'm sorry, he has to go back."

Stella was devastated, but Mrs Tarrant was firmly on

Avery's side. She told Misty's owners in no uncertain terms that the trial was over and they could load him up and take him home because her daughter would not be buying him after all. And so Stella watched in disbelief as her new pony was led straight back on to the float and taken away again.

"I knew it was too good to be true finding a perfect pony that quickly," Stella groaned as she watched Misty being driven off. "Now the rally is just three days away and I don't have a horse to ride."

"Of course you do," was Issie's automatic response. "You can have one of mine."

"What?" Stella's eyes went wide with shock. "You mean it?"

"Totally! I should have suggested it sooner. It's crazy for me to have three horses when there's no way that I can exercise them all at once." She smiled at Stella. "You'd be doing me a favour if you could work one of them. At least until a decent pony turns up for you to buy."

"So which one do you want me to have?" asked Stella.

"Comet," Issie said decisively. "Blaze is too fresh; she's only just coming back into work and she's really sensitive. And I'd love to offload the piebald on you, but I did promise Aunty Hess that I would ride that big black and white lump myself."

"Are you sure?" Stella said, looking slightly awestruck. "Comet is worth a total bomb – he's a superstar showjumper. What if something happens to him?"

Issie shook her head. "You'll be great on him. Besides, Comet may be valuable, but it's not like you have to wrap him in cotton wool – he's pretty tough. He's a Blackthorn Pony, remember?"

"You know," Kate pointed out to Issie, "the piebald is a Blackthorn Pony as well. He's got the same bloodlines as Comet, but it seems like you're convinced he's useless."

Stella agreed. "You are kinda harsh on him, Issie. Maybe you should give him a chance?"

Issie sighed. "I know, I know, but really…" She gestured to the piebald who was, as usual, lying down and snoring in the middle of the paddock, "… look at him! He's a total fruit loop!"

"Well, I think he's adorable," Stella said sniffily. "I've always loved piebalds. I think he looks like one of those horses that pull the painted wagons at carnivals, you know, like a fortune-teller's pony."

Issie looked stunned. "Stella, you're a genius!"

"I am?" Stella had been called a lot of things, but

genius was not one of them. "Umm, OK... why exactly am I a genius?"

"Because," Issie said, "we've all been racking our brains for days now trying to think of a name for this pony and you just said it. He does look like a fortune-teller's pony. *Fortune Teller*. That can be his name! It's perfect for him."

Kate nodded. "Fortune Teller. Yeah, it does suit him. That can be his show name for when he's competing, and then at home you can just shorten it to Fortune."

"Fortune Teller." Stella looked pleased with herself. "It is good, isn't it? I've never come up with a name for a horse before!"

"Well," Kate said, "he's not 'The Piebald' any more. Maybe having a name will help him."

Issie looked at the horse lying on the ground. She wasn't sure it would be enough to make a difference. The piebald was such a kook! She could hear his snoring from the other side of the paddock. "Wake up, Fortune," she said. "You just got yourself a name."

Fortune had been at the River Paddock for almost a week now and Issie hadn't even ridden him. When Stella and

Kate pointed this out she kept coming up with excuses. Blaze was just coming back into work and there was Comet to take care of. But then Issie remembered Aunty Hess's request that she make a prize-winner out of the piebald and she realised she couldn't keep avoiding her responsibilities forever. So on Thursday she headed down to the River Paddock, ready to take her first ride on the new pony.

"We're just going to take it slow," she told Fortune as she slipped the halter on and led him back to the hitching rail by the tack shed. "We'll go on a bit of a hack and get to know each other."

Fortune, for his part, seemed just as unenthusiastic about getting to know Issie. It wasn't like he ran away when she came to catch him, but he didn't rush up to greet her either. He just ignored her. It was the same when she tied him to the hitching rail and began grooming him. Fortune just stared vacantly ahead as she worked over him with a body brush. He barely paid any attention to her at all.

At least he seemed to have no vices. He stood perfectly still, never trying to bite or kick as Issie combed his thick black and white mane and brushed out his long, bushy tail. He picked up his hooves politely, allowing Issie to pick them out with no fuss or bother. "Aunty Hess and Aidan have taught you good manners," Issie told the piebald. Still, she thought when she stepped back from her grooming to assess the pony, he was such a funny-looking thing with his tubby pot belly and gormless expression.

Oh, well, she told herself, *it doesn't matter how he looks, it's how Fortune feels when you ride him that matters.*

It turned out, however, that Fortune felt like a slug. A giant black and white slug. He was completely lethargic and it took all of Issie's efforts just to get the pony moving.

"Come on, Fortune!" Issie was exasperated as she tried to kick the horse into a trot. OK, so Fortune had looked dozy in the paddock, but she had been hoping that once she got on his back that might change. Normally, a horse that had been left unridden for a long time would be full of beans and too peppy. But not Fortune. The piebald was the complete opposite. He was positively nappy and reluctant to budge. Issie found herself resorting to banging her legs repeatedly against the pony's sides like a metronome just to keep him moving forward.

Once he was in motion, Fortune didn't look any more graceful or elegant than when he was standing still.

He stuck his head out in front like a donkey and made grunting noises, his bloated, tubby tummy gurgling away as he trotted. And what a trot! Issie found herself being thrown up in the air out of the saddle like a rag doll. His trot was *so* bouncy, and his belly was so fat her legs stuck out to the sides!

"Maybe we'll just walk again for a bit until we reach the back paddock," she muttered, slowing the pony down. She turned Fortune towards the fenceline and let him proceed at his own treacle-paced walk to the gate that led through to the next paddock.

Despite Fortune's dozy attitude, Issie had still decided it would be safest to stay in the paddock for their first hack today. That way, if Fortune did decide to bolt, at least they would be fenced in. But in truth, Fortune was hardly likely to bolt – it was tough enough getting him to move at all!

Issie didn't mind staying within the grazing grounds. The paddocks by the river were a brilliant place to ride. If you were a pony-club grazing member, you could choose to graze your horse either at the River Paddock or at the main pony-club grounds, but Issie, Stella and Kate liked the River Paddock the best. There wasn't much here in the way of fancy equipment, just a basic outdoor arena with a few cavaletti set up in it. If you wanted to do any serious jumping, you needed to go to the pony club where the jumps equipment was kept. But the girls preferred it. You could hack out to Winterflood Farm along the riverbank or stay in the paddocks like Issie was today and ride through The Pines, a glade of tall conifers at the far end of the back river paddock.

In winter, if it had been raining a lot, the ground in The Pines could be boggy, but otherwise the small woods were perfect for riding. The trees were dense, but there was a well-defined track that ran between them, just wide enough for a horse and rider. The path was carpeted with a blanket of crunchy brown pine needles that gave off a wonderful aroma as you rode through the trees.

When Mystic had been alive Issie loved to ride him here. The Pines had been their special place. Now, as she rode through the gate to the next paddock and turned to head towards the trees on Fortune, she felt a twinge of sorrow as her mind flashed back to thoughts of her beloved pony.

Mystic had been Issie's first ever horse and she had adored him from the moment they met. The swaybacked dapple-grey was hardly the best-looking horse in the paddock at Chevalier Point, but that had never mattered to Issie. To her, Mystic was the most beautiful horse ever. He would always be the horse that she had loved first, the one who had changed everything.

The accident happened at the pony club over two years ago. Issie still had flashbacks to that fateful day. She had turned up at the horse floats just in time to see Natasha Tucker throw a temper tantrum and hit her horse, Goldrush. The palomino had panicked and reared back into Toby and Coco. All three horses had got loose and before Issie could stop to think she was riding after them on Mystic. She managed to herd the escaped horses back from the main road to safety. Then suddenly, it was just Issie and Mystic alone on the road. Issie could hear the low rumble of the truck, smell the diesel and hear the squeal of tyres as the massive vehicle tried to brake. Mystic had turned to face the truck, squaring up to his opponent like a stallion ready to fight. As he reared up the grey pony threw Issie back and out of the saddle. There had been a sickening crack as her riding helmet hit the tarmac, then the taste of blood in her mouth before everything turned to black.

When Issie woke up in the hospital bed her mother was sitting beside her. Issie's first question had been about her horse. "Where is Mystic? Mum? Is Mystic OK?"

Issie still remembered, with awful clarity, that terrible moment, her mother's stilted, painful words. "Isadora, there was nothing anyone could have done… Mystic… Mystic is dead."

Issie truly believed that she would never recover from that moment. Losing her horse was the worst thing that had ever happened to her. She was so devastated she swore that she would never ride again. But then Avery found Blaze. Her instructor worked for the International League for the Protection of Horses and he asked Issie to take on the care of the mistreated mare. Blaze was in a bad way, but together the broken-hearted girl and the broken-spirited horse healed each other.

As for Mystic, it turned out that Issie's bond with her grey pony was so strong that even death could not break it. In fact, Mystic wasn't really gone at all. Whenever Issie was in real trouble and truly needed him, Mystic would be there by her side. He was her guardian angel – not like a ghost, but a real horse, flesh and blood, her protector. The grey gelding had saved her life – and the lives of her horses – so many times. He watched over Issie, Blaze and Storm too. When Storm had needed help in Spain Mystic had been there, and when Issie had to leave the colt behind it helped knowing that somehow Mystic would always be able to keep an eye on him.

The last time Issie had seen Mystic was in the stables of El Caballo Danza Magnifico. That had only been last week, but it seemed so long ago. Now, here she was back at Chevalier Point, riding once again towards the pine trees that Mystic had loved so much. Issie was thinking about the grey gelding, and how much she missed him, so when she saw a grey shadow ahead of her in the trees, she thought she was imagining it. She longed for Mystic to be here with her right now, so perhaps she was seeing things.

It must have been a trick of the light, she decided. But then she saw something that changed her mind. It was the face of a pony. There was no mistaking it this time. There he was, beneath the boughs of a pine tree, staring back at her from the gloom, a snow-white face with a pair of liquid black eyes, peering out from underneath a silvery forelock. The deep, dark eyes looked intently at Issie, meeting her own. Then the horse moved, turning around so that Issie could see his body moving through the branches, a snow-white coat, covered on the rump with a smattering of dark grey dapples. There was no doubt. It was Mystic.

As the grey pony began to move deeper into The

Pines, following the path weaving swiftly between the trees, Issie instinctively clucked Fortune on to follow him. She gave the piebald a swift tap with her heels, urging him to trot and catch up to Mystic. But Issie had forgotten that Fortune wasn't exactly a speedster. Despite the urgency in her voice and the repeated taps on his sides, the piebald pony stubbornly refused to hurry. He gave a grunt as he lurched into a slow trot and then the minute Issie stopped urging him on he fell back into a walk, ambling at a snail's pace.

"Come on, Fortune!" Issie was beside herself with frustration, but it was no use getting worked up. It was already too late. The grey pony had whisked away ahead of them through the pine trees and Issie couldn't see any sign of him. He was gone.

"You stupid piebald!" Issie had never been so angry at a horse. She knew it was wrong to shout at Fortune, but she couldn't help it – she was furious! Mystic had been right there in front of her and because of this stubborn, lazy pony she had lost him! Had Mystic come to warn her of a new danger? Fortune had ruined her chances of finding out. But although Mystic was gone for now, something gave Issie a feeling that this wasn't over yet. He would be back.

CHAPTER 5

Fortune and Comet made a very cute sight together. The piebald and the skewbald were tied up side by side, brown patches next to black patches, by Avery's horse truck waiting for the rally to get under way.

"Don't they look like a matched set?" Stella said. "A bit like salt-and-pepper shakers, similar but not actually the same."

"Trust me, there's nothing even vaguely similar about Comet and Fortune," Issie groaned. After her disastrous ride at the River Paddock she was feeling even gloomier at the prospect of riding the piebald at the pony-club rally today.

Issie hadn't told her friends about what happened at The Pines. How could she when Stella and Kate didn't even know about Mystic? She had told them about Fortune's nappy behaviour on their first ride together though, and how it was impossible to get the pony to listen to her.

"I'm sure Fortune will pep up now that he's at pony club," Stella said optimistically. "He's probably one of those horses who likes an audience. He'll perform in front of a crowd."

The first rally of the new season was a big occasion and the fifty or so riders present were all dressed in the Chevalier Point colours, wearing navy jerseys and red ties. Some of them had even plaited their ponies up for the day – although it wasn't required. Issie, Stella and Kate hadn't bothered to plait, but they were turned out neatly. Stella had even made an effort and shoved her red curls under a hairnet for once. "I got tired of being told off at inspection," she shrugged.

Pony-club rally days always kicked off with inspection. The whole club lined up in front of the clubroom and the instructors passed down the row of horses and riders, checking that tack was clean, safe and done up correctly, that the ponies were groomed properly and the riders' uniforms weren't sloppy.

"It's like being in the army or something," Stella

complained as they lined up. Issie looked down the row of horses and riders. Everyone was lined up straight except for her. "Come on, Fortune!" She gave the piebald a tap with her heels, but he stubbornly refused to move forward the two measly steps needed to line up with the others. Issie sighed. Fortune simply wouldn't listen to her! How was she possibly going to get through an entire rally day on the pigheaded piebald?

Avery cast a glance in Issie's direction, but he didn't seem concerned that she was ruining his straight line. As head instructor it was his job to get the first rally of the season under way. "Lovely to see so many new faces here today," Avery boomed. "We'll be dividing the riders up into four groups. Any new members will be with Jacqui Anderson in the jumping arena. Can you all move off now and follow Jacqui over there?"

Avery waited a moment, giving the new riders a chance to follow their instructor off towards the far arena. Then he turned back to the remaining riders. "All our juniors raise your hands. Excellent! You'll be with Taylor Wilson today, down at the far end of the club in the small arena. Intermediates? You're doing games down in the far paddock with Mandy Jennings. Can you all head off now with your instructors, please? Senior riders, please remain where you are. You'll be with me in the main arena."

The juniors and the intermediate riders peeled off, so that eventually only the Chevalier Point seniors remained. There were ten seniors at the club this season and all of them were present today. There were Issie, Stella and Kate, of course, and Dan and Ben. The Miller sisters, Pip and Catherine, were both back for the season on their matching grey ponies, and Morgan Chatswood-Smith was here today too for the first time in ages, still riding her pony Black Jack. Annabel Willets, having recovered from the broken arm she suffered last season on her palomino, Eddie, was back in the saddle.

At the far end of the row, looking thoroughly bored as usual, was Natasha Tucker. She was mounted on Romeo, her stunningly beautiful Selle Francais. Issie gazed at the handsome chestnut gelding and couldn't help feeling jealous. Romeo shone like a newly-minted copper coin, his glossy coat polished to a perfect sheen, no doubt by one of the grooms at Ginty McLintoch's stables where he was kept. His mane was expertly pulled and Ginty's team must have spent ages that morning making sure that the two socks on his hind legs looked like they had been soaked in Persil – they were so unbelievably white.

Issie had put a fair bit of effort into getting Fortune groomed for today, but no matter how much elbow grease she applied to the piebald he was still a tubby, scruffy pony. How could Issie and Fortune possibly compete with a fancy French-bred hack like that?

The fact that Romeo was the best-looking horse at Chevalier Point certainly hadn't escaped Natasha. She had seen Issie's eyes hungrily admiring him and as Avery's ride began to move off towards the arena she took great pleasure in riding past Issie and muttering under her breath, "That is the ugliest piebald I have ever seen!"

Issie had learnt a long time ago to ignore Natasha's stinging comments, but this one really hurt. She wished that Fortune would step into the arena and teach Stuck-up Tucker a lesson by performing like a superstar. But it just wasn't going to happen. If anything, Fortune's attitude was even worse than his looks. He was nappy and stubborn, plodding forward like a total slow poke.

When Avery asked them to trot Issie had to give him a kick to get him moving and the minute she stopped urging him on with her heels Fortune came to a sudden stop. Issie, who wasn't expecting it, lurched forward and nearly flew over his ears.

"Come on, Fortune... urghh!" Issie gave the piebald

another vigorous tap with her heels. He didn't move.

"Having problems?" Avery asked as he walked over to see what was wrong.

Issie felt her cheeks burning with embarrassment. Here she was, a senior rider, and she couldn't even make her horse trot!

"He was like this the other day in the paddock too. He's being really nappy and he won't do what I tell him to," she admitted.

"Mr Avery?" Natasha called out. "Should Isadora be riding in the senior group if she can't even make that pony trot? We're trying to train for the Tucker Trophy and she's slowing us all down."

Avery took in Natasha's smug smirk. "I'm sure you'll cope, Natasha," he replied flatly. "Just warm up by yourselves for ten minutes," he told the rest of the ride. Natasha sat and glared a bit longer, then she rolled her eyes and rode off to join the other seniors who were warming their horses up at the far end of the ring.

Avery turned his attention back to Issie and Fortune. "Hop off a minute," he said. "I want to double-check that there's nothing wrong with your tack. Fortune might be in pain, which would explain why he's being reluctant."

Issie slid down from the saddle and held Fortune's

reins while Avery worked his way around the pony, checking the fit of the saddle and picking up Fortune's hooves to make sure he didn't have a stone bruise or anything else that might be making him sore.

"Well," Avery assessed, "I can't find anything wrong. This pony seems fine. Apart from the fact he's extremely fat and clearly unfit from lack of work. If you ask me, it's carrying all that extra weight that's causing his nappy attitude."

"Really?" Issie was surprised.

"Absolutely," Avery said. "If you were dreadfully overweight, you wouldn't want to go for a trot either, would you? Being fat is very bad for horses. This horse is so out of shape, he runs the risk of foundering."

"Is that serious?" asked Issie.

Avery nodded. "Very. Overweight ponies can actually die from founder. Fortune needs to lose that tummy of his before he can be a happy, healthy horse."

Avery ran a hand over Fortune's sizeable belly. "Unfortunately, I suspect he's got into this state because he's what you'd call a 'good do-er'."

"What does that mean?" Issie asked.

"It means that Fortune can get fat on the smell of an oily rag." Avery smiled. "He needs to be kept on reduced rations. He must be grazed on limited pasture."

"But how am I supposed to do that?" Issie grumbled. "There's loads of long grass at the River Paddock – how am I going to stop him eating?"

"Graze him here from now on," Avery suggested. "The pony-club paddocks are smaller than the ones at the River Paddock and there's less grass. You should graze him here on short grass for at least the next few weeks while the spring growth is coming through. In fact, if I were you, I'd put him in the parking paddock near the entrance – there's hardly any grass in there at all."

"But won't he starve?" Issie was worried.

"A pony like that? Not a chance!" Avery said. "It's for his own good, Issie. If you keep him on short grass, give him no more than a handful of hard feed and make sure you're doing some conditioning work on him, trotting for at least thirty minutes every day, then you'll have him fit in a matter of weeks."

Issie groaned. "Does it have to be trotting? His trot is awful to ride – it's super-bouncy." Then she added, "That is, when I can actually make him trot at all. He's such a lump."

Avery frowned. "It'll take a while to get him fit, but in the meantime I have the short-term solution to Fortune's sluggish attitude – but you're not going to like it."

"I'll try anything. He's totally impossible."

"Take this then," Avery said. He held out his brown leather riding crop, which he used during lessons – never on horses – to whack against his long riding boots for emphasis when he was making a point to his pupils.

Issie shook her head. "I never carry a whip, Tom. I don't like using them."

"I'm not asking you to use it, Issie," Avery said. "I'm asking you to trust me and take it."

Issie put out her hand and Avery stepped around so that he was standing directly in front of Fortune where the horse could clearly see him. Then he handed Issie the crop in a deliberate manner, as if he was moving in slow motion.

"Do you see what I'm doing here?" he asked. "I want to be certain that Fortune is totally aware of the fact that I'm handing this whip to you."

Issie was puzzled. "Why?"

"Because," Avery explained, "I'm giving you the crop for psychological purposes."

Issie was horrified. "But I don't want to hit him!"

"Shhh," Avery replied. "You and I know that – but Fortune doesn't. It's a mind trick, you see. Often all you need to do is carry a whip. Once a nappy horse knows that you've got it in your hands you won't even need to use it on him."

Issie took the whip from Avery.

"Now," her instructor said, "this time, instead of banging away at Fortune with your ankles to get him to move off, give him one single tap behind your leg with the crop, just to let him know that it's there." Avery was right. The very moment Issie touched Fortune with the whip the piebald responded by stepping forward without any fuss.

"Ohmygod!" Issie couldn't believe it. Fortune's walk was no longer slug-like, but brisk and swingy.

"Now ask him again, reinforcing your leg with a light tap of the crop, and go into trot," Avery said. Issie did as her instructor asked and Fortune moved forward instantly. His trot was still horribly bouncy of course, but at least she could keep her balance now that she didn't have to flap about to make him trot.

"How is he?" asked Avery.

"He's going much better," Issie admitted.

"Excellent," Avery said. "Join the back of the ride and let's get some work done. Rising trot, please, everyone!"

By the end of the lesson, Issie had been given a plan

of action by Avery, who was quite convinced that with lots of road work and a new diet Fortune would become a different horse.

"I'm going to start doing conditioning work tomorrow," Issie told Stella as the girls tied up the horses for lunch break. "Avery says Fortune will have a complete change of personality once he's been on reduced rations."

Stella looked over at Natasha Tucker who had already tied Romeo up and was sitting down to lunch with her mum. "Maybe we should reduce Stuck-up Tucker's rations and see if her personality changes. I heard what she said to you in the arena. What a mega-cow!"

Kate pulled a sour face and did her best Natasha imitation, mocking the bratty blonde's high-pitched voice, *"Some of us are training for the Tucker Trophy, you know."*

The three girls rolled around on the picnic blanket laughing. "Imagine how annoying it's going to be if she actually wins that stupid trophy," Stella pointed out. "I don't think I'll be able to stand being at the same pony club as her."

"The awful thing is, she probably will win it at this rate," Issie groaned. "She's got the best horse."

Issie couldn't help but compare the elegant purebred Romeo, standing handsomely beside Natasha's glamorous silver and blue horse truck, with little fatty Fortune, who was busily snuffling at his hay net like a truffle pig. Maybe Natasha's catty comment at the AGM was true. With a horse like Romeo perhaps she really was out of Issie's league. It hadn't mattered so much when the girls were younger, but now they were at senior level, having a good horse made all the difference. Natasha was cruel – but she might also be right.

Lunch break was over and the afternoon lesson was just about to begin when the new pony-club president arrived. Dressed in a suit, with his Italian loafers freshly polished and gleaming, Oliver Tucker strode across the field towards his daughter.

"Hi, Dad!" Natasha beamed. "You're just in time to watch the jumping. I've got Romeo going really nicely. Watch us do the Show Hunter course."

Oliver Tucker looked at his daughter as if she were a fly buzzing around his sandwich. "Natasha, with the amount of money we spend schooling this beast with Ginty, I'm sure that even a trained monkey could make it jump without messing it up," he said dismissively. "Anyway, I don't have time. I've got business to attend to."

Natasha's face fell as her father turned his back on her and kept walking. He hadn't been looking for his daughter. Tom Avery was his target and he headed towards him, looking like a man on a mission.

"Avery!" he boomed out so that the whole pony club turned around to listen. "We have a *serious* problem."

Tom, who was in the middle of helping Stella to attach a running martingale to Comet's reins, stopped what he was doing and turned to face Mr Tucker.

"And what problem is that, Oliver?"

Mr Tucker reached into his pocket and produced a small, white object. He triumphantly held it aloft for everyone to see. It was a golf ball.

"I found this floating in the horse trough in the middle of the club grounds," he said gravely. "And I think we all know what that means!"

"You're trying to make extra pocket money by finding used golf balls to sell?" Stella offered.

Mr Tucker glared at Stella. This girl must be the red-headed nuisance that Natasha was always complaining about. Why couldn't pony clubs be more like posh schools? Why did they have to let anyone and everyone join in? All these scruffy kids with their badly-bred ponies. No wonder Natasha resented having to mix with them.

"This is no laughing matter, young lady," Mr Tucker continued. "This golf ball is evidence of the dangers this club is living with every single day that it remains here. Do you realise how ridiculous the Chevalier Point Pony Club location is? There's a main road on one side and a golf course on the other!"

Oliver Tucker reached into his pockets again and dramatically produced two more golf balls which he held aloft. "I found both of these within the pony-club grounds," he continued. "They are obviously stray balls hit by golfers into the paddocks."

"I'm sorry, Oliver," Tom Avery said, "I don't understand what you're driving at."

Oliver Tucker drew himself up to his full height. "Good Lord, man. Think! Imagine if a horse ate a golf ball! Or what if a rider was hit by one? This is a very, very serious matter and as your new president I plan to address it urgently!"

"Oliver," said Avery, "the pony club and the golf club have been neighbours for a very long time now and I've never heard of a horse eating a golf ball. As to the matter of stray balls hitting the riders *or* horses, yes, there is a slight risk and we've already taken it up with the manager of the golf course in the past. He wasn't very sympathetic to our plight..."

"Exactly!" Oliver Tucker cut Avery off. "Drastic action is required."

Avery looked nervous. "What do you mean?"

"Given the extreme danger of being located here," Oliver Tucker continued, "as president I will be recommending that we give up the lease on the pony club and move our entire operation to the River Paddock!"

"What?" Avery was shocked. "When?"

"Immediately. The lease is due for renewal in a couple of months. We could pack up and be gone by then."

"Hang on a minute!" Avery was losing his good humour. "Oliver, I'm not at all sure about this. Even if the club committee agrees to your plan, we can't move right now. We have our dressage day here later this month and our Open Gymkhana a few weeks after that. We'd have to wait until after the gymkhana, and it will take an enormous amount of work to move the jumps and equipment, set up new arenas and shift the clubroom."

"Make it happen!" Oliver Tucker demanded. As a property developer this was his catchphrase, and he was very glad of the chance to use it now.

Avery screwed up his face. "What the heck does that mean?"

"It means that I'm president and I'm telling you," Oliver Tucker said firmly, "that after the Open Gymkhana, we pack our bags. The Chevalier Point Pony Club is out of here."

CHAPTER 6

After all those years as a property developer Oliver Tucker knew how to turn on the charm and he could be very convincing. Even though his plan to move the pony club was completely crazy, by the end of the day, most of the riders' parents seemed to be in agreement with him.

It didn't matter that the two clubs had been neighbours for years without any serious incident. Suddenly, Oliver Tucker had everyone believing that the risk of golf-ball strike was a major cause for concern. Parents were scared that their child or pony might be hit by a wayward ball. The club committee was scheduled to meet right after the Open Gymkhana next month and it looked like the members would support giving up the lease and shifting the whole club down to the River Paddock permanently.

As the rally day came to a close and the floats and trucks headed out of the gates bound for home, Issie couldn't help but feel like this might be the end of an era. In two months' time, if Mr Tucker got his way, they would be saying farewell to the Chevalier Point Pony Club grounds for ever.

"It doesn't make sense," Kate grumbled as she mixed up Toby's feed, stirring the chaff and pony nuts together thoroughly with her hands before placing the bin down on the ground in front of the big bay horse. "Nothing has changed. The golf club and the pony club have always been side by side…"

"… and we've never been struck by stray golf balls," Stella added, finishing Kate's sentence. She put Comet's feed bin down on the ground next to Toby's. "So why is it suddenly all a big deal and we have to move? I don't get it."

Issie looked over at Fortune. While Toby and Comet both had generous portions of pony nuts and chaff in their feed bins, poor Fortune was on the first day of his new fitness regime. He had reduced rations – just a handful of sugar beet and a small scoop of chaff for his supper tonight. Also he was being kept in the car park paddock, while Kate and Stella were letting Comet and Toby loose in the pony-club's middle paddock where the grass was thick and lush.

Fortune snuffled up the last of his hard feed and used his big tongue to lick the bottom of the empty feed bin, before bashing it with his hoof as if to say, *please can I have some more!*

"Nice try, Fortune," Issie said, "but you're on a diet, tubby."

Stella watched Comet using his rubbery lips to snuffle up the last scraps in the bottom of his feed bin.

"Toby's finished too," said Kate. "Shall we get going?"

Issie shook her head. "I have to wait until all the cars are gone before I can take Fortune's halter off and let him go. If anyone's left the gate open, he could get out on to the road."

There was only one car still parked in the paddock. It was a cherry-red Ferrari, a flashy two-seater sports convertible.

"Who does it belong to?" Kate asked.

Issie shook her head. "I don't know. Everyone's gone."

"No," Stella corrected her, "there's still someone here. Look – over by the golf-club fence. Who's that?"

The pony club was bordered on one side by the main road, and on the other side a post and wire boundary fence ran between it and the golf course. Over by the fenceline there was a man doing something rather peculiar. He had a wheel on the end of a long broomstick and he was walking back and forth, taking notes in a book as he went.

"It's Mr Tucker," Kate said. "You can tell by the suit."

"Why is he pushing a unicycle?" Stella asked.

"That's not a unicycle," Issie said. "It's a measuring wheel. You use them to measure out distance on the ground. I've seen Avery use one when he's staking out the dressage arenas."

"Well, what's Natasha's dad doing with one?" Kate said.

While the girls had been talking, Mr Tucker had packed up the measuring wheel and walked back towards his Ferrari. He didn't seem to notice their stares as he threw the wheel on to the passenger seat and jumped in, slamming the door behind him. The car lights came on and the tyres of the Ferrari dug into the grass as the car revved up to the pony-club gates. Mr Tucker leapt out again, swung the gates open and was promptly gone in a cloud of dust.

"Hey!" Issie said. "He didn't close the gate after him. That's against club rules."

"Well!" Stella said. "What was all that stuff with the wheel about?"

"I don't know," Issie said darkly. "It's weird though. How come Mr Tucker never, ever came to watch Natasha ride before and now he suddenly seems to be here all the time?"

The troubles at the pony club must have been weighing heavily on Issie's mind because that night she dreamt that she was back at the clubroom. It was a freezing, wintery night and the wind was howling outside, rattling the decrepit weatherboards. Shivering with cold, Issie fumbled for the light switch. The clubroom was pitch-black except for a patch of moonlight that shone in through the window. The beams fell like a spotlight on to the golden Tucker Trophy in the centre of the room. In the shaft of moonlight the golden horse gleamed and shimmered. The horse's turquoise eyes almost seemed to follow Issie around the room.

Issie stood in front of the statue. She reached out a hand to touch its golden surface. Her fingers were almost within reach when the statue let out a loud whinny. Issie shrieked and pulled her hand back. The statue was alive! Then, from the depths of her dream, she heard the whinny again. It was a clarion call, shrill and bellowing, and this time it woke her up so that she sat bolt upright in bed with her eyes wide open. What was going on?

The whinny sounded out again, ringing clear in the night air, and Issie realised that it hadn't been part of her dream. The whinny was quite real and it was coming from outside her bedroom window.

"Mystic!" Issie leapt out of bed and ran to the window. She pressed her nose up against the glass, looking out into the darkness. She could see the shape of a horse on her back lawn. It had to be Mystic. He was waiting for her and he was getting impatient. He let out another loud whinny.

"OK, I'm coming... I'm coming..." Issie muttered as she searched in the dark bedroom for some clothes to put on. She didn't want to switch on the light and risk waking her mum. Then again, if she didn't hurry up, Mystic's whinnies were bound to do the trick anyway.

Luckily, her jodhpurs and boots were still in a heap on the floor where she had thrown them when she got home after the rally. She hurriedly pulled off her pyjama bottoms and yanked the jods on, and then shoved her feet into the boots without bothering with socks. There wasn't time to muck about. Her polar fleece was hanging on the back of her wardrobe door so she grabbed that too as she headed out, tiptoeing down the stairs, ducking out through the kitchen to the French doors that led to the back lawn.

The grey horse was waiting for her. Issie felt her heart beat faster as she saw her beloved grey pony in the moonlight, his coal-black eyes, almost hidden beneath his silvery forelock, were gazing at her intently. Mystic gave a soft nicker, as if to say hello.

"Hey, Mystic, it's so good to see you," Issie breathed softly to her pony. "That was you the other day in The Pines, wasn't it? Why didn't you wait for me? I was trying to follow you, but Fortune was too slow to keep up."

Issie reached out a hand and ran her fingers through the grey gelding's mane, feeling the coarse, ropey fibres against her skin. Even now, after all this time, it was still a shock that her pony was here, that he was real and alive. She could feel the warmth of his soft coat beneath the mane, smell the gentle, warm odour of horse sweat in the cold night air.

Perhaps, Issie thought, seeing Mystic in The Pines

had just been a warning that something was coming. His arrival tonight signalled that the danger, whatever it may be, was far more immediate now. The grey gelding was here to help and his impatience meant that they needed to move fast.

"Mystic…" Issie began, but before she could finish the grey pony had broken away from her and set off back down the lawn towards the wooden gate under the trees at the far end of the garden. The gate was illuminated by a streetlight, so Issie could see to open the latch to let Mystic through.

On the other side of the gate, Issie climbed the bars to get up high enough to make the leap on to her pony's back. With no reins to hold, she buried her hands in the gelding's thick, ropey mane as he set off at a trot along the back street behind Issie's house. His hooves made a clack-clack on the tarmac for a moment before they struck the soft dirt of the grass verge and Mystic began to canter. Issie didn't try to guide him. The grey gelding knew where he was going. All she did was hang on and try to stay low, sheltering from the biting wind by keeping her head down close to Mystic's neck.

The little grey gelding was such a dream to ride that, even when you were bareback, his canter was so fluid and floaty it was like riding a rocking horse. Issie didn't know where they were going or what was going to happen, but she trusted him and felt safe on his back.

As Mystic cantered on down the street Issie felt a chill up her spine. There was an intersection up ahead and, sure enough, when they reached the corner the pony turned right, striking out along the main road that led to the pony club.

In broad daylight this road was nerve-wracking to ride alongside because of the traffic. But now, in the early hours of the morning, there were hardly any cars at all. It wasn't until they had almost reached the turn-off to the pony club that Issie found herself being momentarily blinded by the headlights of a car – coming straight at her! For a moment she panicked that the car was going to hit them, and there was nothing she could do except shut her eyes tight, blocking out the searing white light of the headlights. She wrapped her hands deeper into Mystic's mane and hung on. But the car headlights passed without coming close to them and Mystic kept going at a steady canter, turning down the gravel side road that led to the pony-club grounds.

As Mystic slowed down to a trot near the front gate Issie vaulted to dismount and then dashed forward to find that the padlock was still locked.

"Wait for me here," she hissed at Mystic. "I'll be back in a minute." The grey pony stamped his feet anxiously as he watched her clamber over the fence and leap down into the car park paddock on the other side.

As she walked across the paddock she realised that, although Mystic had brought her to the pony club, she didn't actually know why she was here. She had no idea what the danger was, or why Mystic had come to her. Issie looked around. The night was totally quiet and there was no sign of anyone else lurking about. She decided that the logical thing to do would be to check all the horses first and then…

A noise behind her made her jump. Terrified, she spun around, then leapt back in shock. "Mystic!" she cried. "Ohmygod! You gave me a fright. Don't scare me like that!"

Then Issie looked back at the gate. It was still locked. "How did you get in here?" she whispered to the grey pony. Mystic gave a nicker and wheeled about on his hocks heading towards the far side of the paddock at a brisk trot. Issie ran behind him, following the grey pony's shadowy shape in the darkness until they reached the fenceline that divided the pony club from the golf course.

Issie expected Mystic to stop, but the grey gelding put on a sudden surge of speed, cantering straight ahead – right through the wire fence!

Issie couldn't believe her eyes. But as she came closer she realised that there was a big gap in the fence – a whole chunk of wire and wooden palings had been cut away with wire snips and bent back, leaving a huge, horse-sized hole.

It took a second for the next realisation to hit home and then Issie's blood ran cold. If the hole was big enough for Mystic to fit through then it was big enough for Fortune to escape from as well. She had left the piebald grazing alone in this paddock when she went home. Now, as she looked around frantically in the darkness, she realised she couldn't see him anywhere. He must have got out through the hole in the fence. Fortune was loose and he was somewhere out there on the golf course!

"Mystic?" Issie called as she stepped through the hole. She peered desperately into the blackness in front of her. "Fortune?" she called hopefully. There was no reply from either of them. Ahead of her the golf course stretched out endlessly; shadowy clusters of trees and the gloomy outlines of sand bunkers, hills and hollows were barely visible in the dark night. There were no fences here to contain a piebald pony. Fortune could be all the way over on the other side of the course by now. It would be impossible to find him.

"Fortune!" Issie felt panic rising in her. She was about to put her fingers to her lips and whistle when she heard a horse whinny, and then a second horse returning the call. The first whinny had come from Mystic. He had found Fortune, right beside the pony-club fence, less than ten metres from the hole! The two ponies were standing happily side by side. Mystic was looking at Issie with wise, dark eyes. Fortune had popped his head up briefly to whinny and now had his snout back down in the long grass, grazing like mad.

Issie breathed a sigh of relief. For once Fortune's gluttony had worked in her favour. The pony must have escaped through the gap and spotted the long grass by the fence that the mower couldn't reach. He was so keen to get his head down and eat that he hadn't strayed very far at all.

"Hey, Fortune," Issie said to the piebald. "Turns out the grass really is greener on the other side of the fence."

She looked at Mystic. "Can you keep an eye on him while I get his halter?" she asked the grey gelding.

Mystic seemed happy enough to babysit and when Issie came back Fortune was exactly where he had been before, with his head down, tucking into the long grass. She slipped the halter easily over his head and led the piebald back through the gap in the fence and into his paddock again.

Once Fortune was safely inside, she tied him up then went back to the pony-club sheds and grabbed a couple of painted poles that were used for jumping. She propped these up lengthwise, across the front of the hole, to serve as a makeshift barrier.

"That should stop you escaping until we can fix it properly tomorrow," she told Fortune.

Fortune didn't look at all pleased about having his midnight feast curtailed. When Issie slipped his halter off he went over to the rails and gave them a sniff, as if he was disappointed that his escape had been thwarted.

"Thank goodness you're such a greedy pony," Issie said. Whoever had cut the hole in the fence tonight must have expected Fortune to race off. She might never have found him if Fortune hadn't listened to his tummy and paused to eat. Issie looked hard at the hole in the fence. The wires had been deliberately cut and the palings had been pulled away. There was no way this was an accident. Someone had wanted Fortune to get out tonight. But why?

CHAPTER 7

When Avery arrived the next morning with some number eight wire to fix the hole in the fence he was shocked by the size of it.

"When you told me the fence needed mending I was expecting a broken strand or two," he told Issie. "Look at the way the wire's been cut and bent back. It's definitely been done on purpose."

Avery put down his tool kit and walked through the hole to examine the state of the golf green. "It doesn't look too bad," he said. "If you hadn't caught Fortune as quickly as you did, he could have badly damaged the golf course."

"I thought you'd be worried about the horse, not the grass," Issie said.

Avery sighed. "Under normal circumstances yes, but not when you're dealing with Gordon Cheeseman."

"Who's Gordon Cheeseman?"

"The golf-club manager. He absolutely loathes the pony club. He's had it in for us for years, looking for any excuse to start yet another war with the pony-club committee. All we'd need is hoof prints on one of his precious putting greens and he'd go ballistic."

"Lucky for us then that Fortune is such a greedy pig and just headed for the long grass," Issie said.

Avery frowned at this comment then opened up his tool kit, selecting a wire tightener and getting to work on the fence.

"So," Issie continued, "who do you think has done this?"

Avery pondered this question as he worked. "Vandals perhaps, trying to let horses loose on the golf course as some kind of stupid joke. Or maybe it was someone who was planning to steal a horse? It wouldn't be the first time, would it?"

Issie shook her head. "I can see why they'd want to steal Blaze or Comet, but I can't imagine anyone in their right mind wanting to steal Fortune."

Avery stopped work and turned to look at Issie. "You know, that's the second time in this conversation that you've insulted Fortune. In fact, come to think of it, I haven't heard you say a single positive thing about that piebald since he got here. I imagine you think it's funny, making jokes about him, but I think there's something more serious going on here, don't you?"

"What do you mean?" Issie was taken aback. Avery seemed really serious.

"I heard you talking about Fortune at the rally day too," he continued, "making jokes about him. You run him down all the time, Issie. It's clear you don't like him."

"It's not that!" Issie defended herself. "I don't mean to be like that. It's just, well… look at him! He's not a star like Comet or Blaze, is he? He's totally nutty. All he seems to want to do is eat and sleep. Besides, Aunty Hess just dumped him on me and he's—"

Avery cut her off. "I know you didn't ask to be given the responsibility of training Fortune. But you agreed to take him on when Aidan brought him here, and now you have to do that, for Fortune's sake." Avery paused. "You know, I seem to recall that when I brought Blaze to you and asked you to look after her, she wasn't exactly in top condition either. So why aren't you treating Fortune the way you treated her?"

"I don't know," groaned Issie. "It's just such bad timing. I've already got two horses – I don't need another. If I want to win the Tucker Trophy, I should really be focusing on Comet or Blaze. I don't stand a chance on Fortune."

"Is that really what's worrying you?" Avery said. "Winning that trophy?"

Issie nodded. "I know I shouldn't care about it, but Natasha has been winding me up no end. It's all right for her. She has her really expensive sport-horse and I've been lumbered with this crazy piebald. He's going to ruin my chances of winning."

Avery shook his head in disbelief. "Issie, don't you realise you have a special opportunity with this horse?"

"What do you mean?"

"Sure, it's easy to look good when you have a horse like Romeo – there's no challenge. But if you can take a horse like Fortune and put the work in and turn him into a performance sport-horse, that's the mark of a real rider," Avery said.

"I've seen brilliant riders take a $200 horse that was on its way to the knacker's yard and turn it into a grand prix showjumper. A great rider can turn the worst problem horse into a champion." Then he added, "I've also seen riders like Natasha, who take a perfectly good horse and turn it sour by treating it badly. She might succeed on that horse for a while, but eventually her attitude will cause problems."

At that moment Issie saw clearly what Avery was driving at. How many horses had Natasha been through since she'd joined the Chevalier Point Pony Club? There had been Goldrush, then Fabergé and now Romeo. They were all brilliant when they arrived at Chevalier Point. They were the sort of horses that Issie dreamt of owning. But Natasha was never happy with any of them. Right from the start, she blamed them for her own faults as a rider and so the horses became worse until she gave up and sold them on.

Issie looked at Fortune, grazing happily at the other side of the paddock. How could she have been so heartless? She had been acting like Natasha towards the piebald from the moment he arrived, and Avery was right: it really wasn't funny. OK, so Fortune was a bit peculiar, but had Issie given him a chance to prove how special he was too? She had the chance to make or break this horse. Issie needed to change her attitude if she was going to help Fortune.

She nodded. "I guess we got off on the wrong foot."

Avery nodded. "Lucky for you he has four of them, so I think there's a chance you can start again." Avery gave the last wire a twist as he finished his fix-up job and then began to pack up his tool kit.

"Why don't we start straight away?" he suggested. "I've arranged with Stella and Kate to meet me here at midday for a dressage lesson. Why don't you saddle Fortune up and join in too?"

Issie smiled gratefully at her instructor. "That sounds like just what we need, Tom."

There was a grunt from the far side of the field as Fortune stopped grazing and dropped down to the ground for his mid-morning nap.

Issie shook her head and grinned. OK, so the piebald had some quirks, but who cared? There was a star buried somewhere in that pony and now she was determined to make it shine.

When Stella and Kate arrived at the club they were very excited by the news of Fortune's bid for freedom.

"It wasn't much of a getaway," Issie admitted as she saddled up. "He only went a couple of metres and then he gave up and decided to eat instead."

"It's weird though," Kate said. "Who would cut a hole in the pony-club fence?"

"Ohmygod!" Stella suddenly froze. "Morgan is back at the club this season. Now she's in the running for the trophy, maybe she's gone off the deep end again?"

Issie shook her head. "I don't think so. Morgan is totally over that whole thing and besides, if anything went wrong, she knows that she'd be the first person we'd suspect. Also it doesn't make sense. If you wanted to win the Tucker Trophy, you'd sabotage Natasha's horse, not Fortune. He's the least likely to win it."

As soon as the words came out of her mouth, Issie realised she was running her horse down again without even thinking about it.

"I'm sorry, Fortune," she said, speaking sincerely to the piebald. "I didn't mean that you won't win. I just meant you're an outside chance." She stroked the pony gently on his Roman nose. "But we'll show them, won't we?"

Fortune gave a grunt of pleasure as Issie stroked him and then took the opportunity to get closer and loll his head over Issie's shoulder, using her as a leaning post.

"Look at him!" Issie giggled. "He'll probably fall asleep like that and start snoring in a minute."

"Aw," Stella said. "Look at you two! New best friends!"

Issie shrugged. "You could say that. Fortune and I are making a fresh start."

The piebald and Issie had made friends, but that didn't mean Fortune had miraculously transformed into the perfect horse. When the three girls began their lesson he was still nappy at first, refusing to move forward. But as Avery instructed Issie, asking her to work her legs more on the piebald, and create impulsion, he began moving forward much more freely.

"More leg, Issie!" Avery insisted. "This horse needs firm aids. Give him a constant push," Avery called out as they worked around the arena. "Blaze and Comet are both naturally very 'forward' horses; they've got so much pep you don't need to use as much leg on them. But Fortune requires more effort from you. Adapt your riding style to suit your horse."

At that moment, it clicked. Issie realised that she hadn't been changing her style at all. Blaze and Comet were both highly-strung tearaways, whereas Fortune was a slow and solid mover. He needed the encouragement of clear, firm aids and plenty of leg to get him moving briskly.

Issie began to rethink her riding, trying to tailor her technique to suit her horse. Instead of giving girly little kicks with each stride, she clamped her leg on really firmly, asking the piebald to step through underneath her. It was like a light bulb had been switched on and Fortune responded instantly. His trot became loose and light and his neck arched so that he looked less like a donkey and more like a show horse. His powerful hindquarters finally engaged and his canter became uphill and elegant as he moved.

"Much better, Isadora!" Avery called out to her. "Now you're really working him. Good stuff!"

"Good boy, Fortune!" Issie patted the black and white pony on his broad neck. They were making progress together at last.

The lesson was so good that Issie wished she could have rewarded Fortune with a big bucket of pony nuts. But Avery was firm and insisted that Fortune received his diet handful of sugar beet and chaff.

"Poor Fortune," Issie said as she watched the piebald hungrily craning his neck over the fence towards Toby and Comet, who were still chomping their way through enormous suppers.

"It's for his own good," Avery insisted. "You need to

start his trotting work too. A daily vigorous half-hour trot, remember, and no matter what, no walking. You have to get this horse moving to get rid of that belly."

"He was already going much better today though, wasn't he? He looked really great in the ring," Issie said.

Avery agreed. "You had him going nicely in there, Issie."

Issie looked embarrassed. "You were right, Tom… about it being my fault before. I guess I lost perspective and…"

But Avery wasn't listening to her. He was staring over Issie's shoulder with a quizzical expression. "Hello," he said. "What's he doing over here?"

A man was standing in the exact spot where Avery had fixed the wire this morning. He was short, bald and rather pink-faced, dressed in a traditional golfer's outfit – a pair of checked plus fours worn with pink socks up to the knee, a pink polo shirt and a matching tam-o'-shanter hat with a pink fluffy bobble on the top. He looked utterly ridiculous and his behaviour was even more curious than his outfit. He kept staring at the fenceline and then bending down with his face right up against the grass as if he were sniffing the ground like a tracker dog.

"Oh, great," Avery groaned. "Here we go again!"

Issie was confused. "Do you know him?"

"Unfortunately, yes," Avery sighed. "That's Gordon Cheeseman, manager of the Chevalier Point Golf Club."

As Avery said this the man looked up and saw him. He gave Avery a brisk wave that was more of a shake of his fist than a friendly greeting. Then he clambered over the wire fence in his voluminous plus fours and began to stride across the pony-club grounds towards them.

"Good afternoon, Gordon," Avery called to him.

"I can't see what's good about it, Avery," the man in the pink-bobbled hat snapped back.

"Is there a problem?"

"You know jolly well there is!" Gordon Cheeseman bit back. "Don't think you can fool me. I know your horses are responsible."

"Responsible for what?" asked Avery.

"Churning up the grass on my golf course," Mr Cheeseman bellowed. "One of your horses has left hoof prints on the green at the eighteenth hole."

Avery turned to Issie. "I thought you said Fortune hadn't wandered far?"

Issie shrugged. "He hadn't. He was next to the fenceline when I found him. I guess he might have trodden on the very edge of the green."

Avery turned back to Mr Cheeseman. "Gordon, how many hoof prints exactly did you find on your green?"

"Three!" Mr Cheeseman announced, his face puce with rage.

"Three?" Avery was trying to remain straight-faced. "You're in a state because of three hoof prints?"

"It might just be three hoof prints to you and your larrikin riders," Mr Cheeseman fumed, "but it has ruined the state of the eighteenth green. I've seen the patch-up job you've done on that fence too, so don't tell me you don't know that a horse escaped last night."

"Gordon," Avery said, "we are victims of the vandals just as much as you are. The fence had been cut clean through with wire snips and one of our horses got out. Luckily, we caught him before any real damage occurred and thankfully the horse is fine."

"The horse?" Mr Cheeseman sputtered with rage. "I don't give a toss about your horse!"

"Then you'll forgive me if I don't care much about the state of your golfing green," Avery said coolly. "As you rightly pointed out I have fixed the fence – which is shared between the pony club and the golf club. I will of course be forwarding your half of the repair costs on to you, Gordon, and I would appreciate prompt payment. Wire doesn't come cheap, you know, and neither does my time."

Gordon Cheeseman's eyes narrowed. "You think you're being funny, don't you, Avery? Well, I've had enough. This is the last straw. I am no longer willing to put up with your pony club. I will be taking this matter to the district council. Your lease is coming up for renewal – let's see whether you can keep your club grounds once I've lodged an official complaint against you!"

And with that, the mad golfer strode off in a huff. His dramatic departure was slightly marred when he stepped in a pile of Fortune's poo in his sparkling white golf shoes.

"Don't laugh, you'll make matters worse," Avery admonished the girls, but he couldn't help smiling as he watched Gordon Cheeseman stomp away.

"Does he mean it?" Kate asked. "About telling the council on us?"

Avery nodded. "I'm sure he does. It's exactly the opportunity Gordon's been waiting for. He's been trying to get rid of us for years."

Suddenly, no one was laughing. This time, it looked like Gordon Cheeseman might actually succeed.

CHAPTER 8

Avery called Issie and Stella the next day and asked the girls if they were able to come over after school to help him out with something. He was very vague about details so the girls got a bit of a surprise when they arrived at Winterflood Farm and he introduced them to three more new horses in the paddock.

There was a very pretty palomino named Lulu and two matching strawberry roans called, rather unimaginatively, Roanie and Strawberry. "Don't blame me," Avery said, "I didn't name them. Aidan did."

"Aidan?" Issie said. "They're from Blackthorn Farm?"

Avery looked surprised. "I thought you knew. That was why I didn't bother with details on the phone. I assumed Aidan had already called you."

Issie looked embarrassed. Aidan hadn't called her. In fact, she hadn't spoken to him since that uncomfortable scene in the kitchen a week ago. "He didn't call me. I didn't even know he'd been here," Issie admitted.

"He still is," Avery said. "He's going to be moving in with me for a few weeks while we school up the horses."

"What?" Issie couldn't believe it. "Where is he now?"

"In the kitchen making us all some afternoon tea."

Issie stomped towards the house with Stella following hot on her heels. She couldn't believe it. Aidan was supposed to be her boyfriend and now she had found out that he hadn't even let her know he was moving in with Tom!

Aidan's face lit up when he saw Issie in the kitchen doorway. "Hey…" he started cheerfully, but then he took in Issie's frown.

"Is there something wrong?"

"Something wrong?" Issie was furious. "Why didn't you tell me you were coming to stay? You said you were going to call me, but you never did!"

"Don't you want me to be here? Is that it?" Aidan looked hurt.

"No! I mean yes, I do want you to be here." Issie suddenly felt embarrassed to be talking like this in front of Stella. "It's just that I wish you would tell me stuff. I mean, you turn up out of the blue and I didn't even know you were coming and then Avery tells me you're staying! I thought you were really busy at the farm."

"I was," Aidan said, "but I've got Bill Stokes from down the road covering for me. He's feeding Butch and Blossom and the ducks. Hester has the rest of the horses with her on the film set. Lulu, Roanie and Strawberry are the remaining ponies coming up for auction. I'm going to stay around for a few weeks with the horses and school them with Avery to get them ready for the sales."

"Well," Issie harrumphed, "you could have told me first. I felt pretty stupid finding out from Tom."

"I should have told you? Yeah, right! Like the way you told me that you were going to Spain?" Aidan shot back. "Issie, I didn't even know you were going and then I get an email and you're at El Caballo Danza Magnifico!"

"That was different," said Issie defensively. "That was..."

"Why was it different? Because I'm supposed to call you even though you never call me?" Aidan said. "Man, I don't believe you, Issie. I go to all this effort to uproot my whole life and move the horses here just so I can spend some time with you, and you're angry because I surprised you? I can't win!"

"Aidan…" Issie began. But it was too late. Aidan had stormed off towards the stables in a fury, leaving Issie standing bewildered in his wake.

Stella and Issie stood there for a moment in silence, and then Stella turned to Issie. "So, your boyfriend's back then?" she grinned. "You must be pleased."

"Don't push your luck, Stella," Issie snapped. "It's not funny."

Issie didn't get it. Aidan was angry at her? He had to be kidding! She was the one who was angry at him! It wasn't her fault she hadn't called before she left for Spain. Everything had happened so fast when Storm was stolen – she didn't get the chance.

But now it seemed like Aidan thought that she didn't care about him. Of course she did! She had been so happy to see him that day he turned up in her kitchen, then he'd dropped the bombshell about Fortune and left again. Issie had started to think that maybe he didn't want to hang around because he didn't want to be her boyfriend any more. So when he turned up again out of the blue, she didn't know what to make of it. Issie groaned. The whole thing was just a disaster. Was Aidan still her boyfriend or not?

When Issie got home she spent the rest of that evening staring at the telephone, willing it to ring. She wanted Aidan to call and tell her it was all a big misunderstanding and that everything was OK. Three hours later, when the phone had refused to ring, she thought about picking it up herself and calling him. But then she got cold feet. What if Aidan didn't want to speak to her? He had been pretty mad when he stormed off. Maybe it was over and he didn't know how to tell her?

She went to bed that night unable to stop thinking about Aidan. She thought about how his dark fringe hid those gorgeous pale-blue eyes, how cute he looked in his jeans and the faded old tartan shirts he always wore. She felt totally miserable that they might be splitting up.

By the next morning, however, Issie had pulled herself together. She was being ridiculous, she decided, moping about, waiting for the phone to ring.

Get over it, she told herself firmly. As of this moment she was going to put Aidan out of her mind and the best way to do that was to focus her energies on her horses.

Avery had written out a rigid exercise regime to get

Fortune into shape. Issie was supposed to hack the piebald out on a road ride each day with thirty minutes of non-stop trotting. And so, the day after her fight with Aidan, Issie headed for the pony-club paddocks after school with big plans for kick-starting the piebald's new healthy workout regime.

Fortune was lying down under one of the magnolia trees in his paddock, snoring as usual, when she arrived. This time when he saw her, the horse actually bothered to get up, clambering inelegantly to his feet.

"Well," Issie said to the piebald as she slipped his halter on, "at least you seem to know who I am now."

Fortune eagerly snuffled up the carrot that the girl offered him. He was hungry. He had been in the short-grass paddock for a few days now and his belly had already lost some of its grass bloat.

"We're going for a big trot today, Fortune, to get you fit," Issie told the piebald. Her plan was to ride him at a walk down the verge of the main road until they reached the back roads that led to the River Paddock. Once they were on the back roads, they would be able to trot on the grass verges. They could keep up a steady pace all the way past the River Paddock until they reached Winterflood Farm. Then they would turn around and trot back again.

Issie figured that would be at least half an hour of non-stop trotting – just what Avery had ordered.

The excursion didn't start well. Fortune was back to his old nappy ways. But Issie was firm with him and gave him a light wave with the stick as Avery had shown her, and the piebald soon knew she meant business.

Once he was out on the open road, Fortune almost seemed to be enjoying himself. His head was raised up high and his ears swivelled back and forth as he listened to Issie's endless stream of conversation. Issie always liked to talk to her horses, using her voice to make them relax. However, today her voice wasn't calming at all. It was squeaky and high-pitched as she carried on a non-stop rant. Poor Fortune was getting a total earful about just how stupid boys were!

"… and then he has the nerve to say that he was only trying to surprise me!" Issie told Fortune. "What does that mean? Why didn't he tell me he was coming? Why does he have to turn up without warning like that?"

Beneath her, Fortune swivelled his ears back and forth as he listened intently. He gave a grunt which could easily have been interpreted as a sympathetic "there-there".

The ride continued like this for the next ten minutes as they headed down the main road. When they finally turned into the side road, with wider grass verges and less traffic, Issie stopped talking so much and began to focus on riding, urging Fortune on into a steady trot. Once again, the piebald was a little bit nappy at first, but then he trotted on, his springy paces throwing her up and down in the saddle as they bounced together down the road.

It was a perfect day to be out riding. The grey skies had cleared and it was one of those fresh, early spring days when the sun isn't too hot on your skin. Everything was going brilliantly until they reached the T-junction at the corner of the road and turned down the esplanade that led towards the River Paddock.

Ahead of them, coming in the opposite direction, also at a trot, was another horse and rider. Issie kept on trotting, smiled and waved a friendly hello at a distance, then a few moments later her face dropped as the horse and rider drew closer and she realised who they were. Marmite and Aidan!

Aidan smiled and waved back to Issie, then clucked Marmite on, heading towards her. When the two horses were just a few metres away from each other Aidan slowed down to a halt, clearly expecting Issie to do the same. His smile faded as he realised that Issie wasn't slowing down at all. She kept trotting straight past Aidan as if he wasn't even there.

"Hey!" Aidan said. "Wait! I want to talk to you. Issie! I want to talk about what happened yesterday at the farm."

"Sorry," Issie called back over her shoulder as she sped on, "I can't stop. Avery told me I have to do thirty minutes of non-stop trotting on Fortune to get him into shape. If you want to talk to me, you better keep up."

Aidan sighed. Why did Issie have to be like this? She was so infuriating! Undaunted, he pivoted Marmite around on his hindquarters and urged the brown pony into a vigorous trot. Within a minute they had caught up to Issie and Fortune. Now the two riders were side by side on the grass verge, Marmite and Fortune keeping perfect stride with each other as they trotted on.

"OK," said Issie, "what did you want to say?"

"Me?" Aidan said. "I thought maybe you might want to say something, Issie. In fact, I was expecting you to call me last night."

Issie was feeling so uncomfortable now she couldn't bring herself to look at Aidan; instead, she looked straight ahead as she rode. "I really wanted to call you," she said, "but I thought you didn't want to speak to me."

"Issie! Don't be ridiculous!"

"Oh!" Issie was insulted. "So now I'm being ridiculous? Listen, Aidan, I understand if you don't want to go out with me any more, but there's no need to be mean."

"Don't want to go out with you?" Aidan was confused. "I thought you didn't want to go out with me! I get one lousy postcard and you don't even call me when you get back, and all your emails from Spain went on about some guy called Alfonso…"

Issie couldn't believe it. "You're jealous of Alfonso?" she said.

"No!" said Aidan. Then he reconsidered his answer. "OK, yes. I'm jealous. I admit it! Happy now?"

"Aidan, that's nuts! Alfie is my friend. You're my *boyfriend!*"

Aidan groaned. "How am I supposed to know that if you don't tell me? You never called me before you left…"

"Hello! My colt had been stolen!" Issie said. "And I know I should have called you when I got back home, but I felt so miserable about leaving Storm in Spain, I didn't want to phone you up and burst into tears."

Aidan looked at her and shook his head. "Issie, that's what I'm here for. You should have told me what you were going through. I just want to be there for you and help you."

"Really?"

"Totally! Why do you think I turned my life upside down to be here? I miss you so much! Issie, I just want things to be the way they were before."

"Well, that's all I want too!" said Issie. She had been keeping Fortune trotting this whole time and the piebald was striding out nicely as she posted up and down.

"Then you're still my girlfriend?" Aidan asked.

Issie felt the flutter of butterflies in her tummy. "I'm still your girlfriend," she smiled.

Aidan rode Marmite closer to Fortune now, trying to keep in stride as the two horses trotted on.

"Umm, Issie?" he said.

"Yeah?"

"Can we stop trotting? Just for a minute?"

Issie shook her head. "Uh-uh. Tom said I have to do thirty minutes of non-stop trot to get Fortune fit. It's only been twenty minutes so far. I can't stop."

"OK then," Aidan said, smiling at the stubbornness of his girl. "I guess I don't have a choice. I'm going to have to do this your way."

He rode Marmite even closer to Fortune, so that his

knees were bumping against Issie's.

"Hey!" Issie said. "You're too close. What are you doing?"

"Giving my girlfriend a kiss," announced Aidan. And with that, he leant over as he rose out of the saddle with a swift bounce and the next thing Issie knew Aidan's lips had connected with her own in the briefest, most fleeting of kisses. Then they were both trotting on once more and Aidan pulled Marmite away so that the horses weren't squashed up against each other.

"This is my stop," he said, gesturing to the turning up ahead that led to Winterflood Farm. "I'll see you later, OK? Maybe we can go to the movies tonight? Pick you up at eight?"

Issie, who was still in shock from the kiss, and the crazy way it had happened, just nodded dumbly. When she reached the corner she turned around and headed the same way she had come, back up the road again towards the pony club. It wasn't until she reached the main road that her heart stopped pounding and she finally thought about what had just happened. She had just broken up with her boyfriend, had a huge fight, kissed and got back together again – and she hadn't stopped trotting the whole time!

CHAPTER 9

Ever since their kiss, Issie and Aidan had seen each other almost every day. They often trained their horses together at Winterflood Farm when Issie got home after school. Issie would trot Fortune all the way to Winterflood Farm to meet Aidan and then ride back to the pony-club paddocks again as part of the pony's fitness workout.

Issie's determination to stick to Avery's exercise regime was definitely paying off. Not only was Fortune's belly shrinking with each passing day, the pony's attitude had improved too. He was much less nappy and his manners under saddle had improved enormously.

Some things about the piebald hadn't changed of course. Fortune was a very oddball character. He never went without his afternoon nap and when Issie arrived at the paddocks after school she would find Fortune lying down fast asleep under the magnolia tree. Issie knew the bond between them had grown because the piebald no longer ignored her and kept sleeping. Instead, he would raise his head, prick up his ears and then clamber to his feet with a grunt, before coming over to the gate to greet her with a merry nicker. Issie had taken to bringing him peppermints and Fortune loved them. He would hold the tiny mints in his mouth and suck on them, shaking his head up and down with delight.

"You're a total kook," Issie would say. But now when she said it, she meant it in a good way, with a broad grin on her face. Issie's attitude to the piebald had totally changed. Regular lessons over the past two weeks with Avery had really helped, and she now understood how to take control when she was riding this horse. Fortune was inclined to daydream and it was up to Issie to keep his mind on the job, always moving him up to the bridle, asking him to pay attention to her legs. Her aids had grown stronger from the work she had been doing and although she still carried the whip, she no longer needed it.

It was about two weeks after Fortune's workouts

began that Avery started to incorporate some jumping training into the piebald's lessons. Issie would trot Fortune to Winterflood Farm and by the time she arrived the piebald would already be nicely warmed up and ready to start jumping.

Avery started with the basics at first, trotting poles and cavaletti. But Fortune was a Blackthorn Pony and his natural jumping bloodlines meant that he soon progressed to small jumps, popping over painted rails with ease. Within the first week, Avery was erecting decent-sized showjumping courses for the pair and they were tackling them with ease. Fortune was never nappy when he was jumping – he loved it! He was almost too eager when he approached the fences and Issie had to hold him back.

"Look how his ears prick forward when he sees a fence," Avery pointed out during a lesson one day. "He reminds me of the first time I saw you on Comet."

Fortune had the same scopey jump as the skewbald too. But he was still green and Avery explained to Issie how important it was to give him loads of experience jumping all kinds of fences. Each day, when Issie turned up at Winterflood Farm, she would find a new obstacle set up that she had never seen before. On

Monday it was 44-gallon drums painted bright blue. On Tuesday Avery had strung old car tyres over a log. And so the week went on until Friday came and Issie arrived to find a full wire hunting fence set up in the middle of the ring.

The wire fence was the size of a normal jump. It stood about a metre-twenty high, and looked just like the wire-and-post fence that ran around a pony paddock. The wooden palings which ran vertically through the wire were painted white and the wire itself was just regular number eight wire.

"You've never seen one of these before?" Avery asked.

Issie shook her head.

"It's a common jump in round-the-ring or Show Hunter classes," Avery said. "Show Hunter classes are designed to resemble the kinds of natural obstacles that you'll find if you're out riding in a hunt. You get gates, brush fences and wire fences like this one. They're jazzed up a bit for the show ring of course – the wooden bits get painted white."

Issie looked at the wire fence and pulled a face.

"Something wrong?" asked Avery.

"It looks dangerous," Issie admitted. "The wire is so thin. How do horses see the wire and know to jump it?

Won't they just crash into it and slice their legs or something?"

Avery shook his head. "Don't worry, there are wire fences like this when riders go out hunting and the horses have no trouble with them."

Issie didn't know what to say. Avery seemed very certain – but the jump looked so lethal!

"How do I approach it?" she asked.

"Just like any other fence. It's a new obstacle so come in slowly and give Fortune a chance to have a bit of a look and then just pop him over it."

Avery glanced around the arena. "We'll set up a bit of a course for you to ride first and then you can do the wire last."

The course that Avery constructed consisted of a few of the obstacles that Issie had already jumped Fortune over. There were 44-gallon drums, tyres, a hog's back of red and white painted rails, a white painted gate, and finally, in the centre of the ring, stood the wire.

"Take him around the outside circuit once first without doing the wire," Avery told Issie as she warmed Fortune up, trotting him in a twenty-metre circle. "Then do it a second time and jump the wire."

Fortune's bouncy trot eased into a loping canter as

Issie rode the piebald around the warm-up circle, ready to take him over the first fence. She leant forward – but not too far. She wanted to keep her bottom in contact with the saddle just in case she needed to really urge the piebald on. As they approached the oil drums Issie checked Fortune's stride, then let him go and put her legs on right in front of the jump. The piebald did a lovely take-off and they landed on the other side with Issie already looking to their next fence. The piebald stood back a bit at the tyre jump, but Issie put her legs on more firmly and sat down a little to make sure Fortune obeyed her aids and he jumped neatly once again. He had no trouble with the red and white hog's back and positively flew over the gate before coming back to Avery.

"Very nice," Avery said. "You could have done with a bit more impulsion coming into that tyre jump, but otherwise, very good. Now let's try it again and this time, take him over the wire as the last fence in the course."

As Issie did the warm-up circle before the first jump things felt different somehow. She had butterflies – which was nothing new – but this time, they didn't feel like butterflies. They felt like worms, writhing about, making her feel sick with anxiety. She looked over at the wire fence and the worms began to wriggle even harder.

"You should be looking at the first fence!" Avery called out to her. "Concentrate on where you're going."

Issie nodded and pushed Fortune on into a canter. As the pony bore down on the oil drums for the second time there was no hesitation in his stride and Issie let him judge his own pace, keeping her legs on for the last two strides just to urge him over. She kept Fortune's canter rhythm steady coming into the tyres so that he popped over much more neatly, and he made a lovely job of the hog's back.

This time, as they flew over the white gate, instead of preparing to pull him up, Issie kept her canter steady and turned to look at the wire fence. She looped Fortune around the edge of the ring, aiming him at the fence nice and straight, with room for at least six strides as they approached the wire. She was still quite far back when she decided she needed to speed up to get over the jump and urged Fortune on.

As his stride got faster Fortune began to realise that this jump was different. He began to fret, lifting his head above the bit. The whites of his eyes began to show as he boggled at the wire ahead of him and his canter became disunited and wobbly. As Fortune began to pull against Issie's hands she snatched at the reins, trying to keep him under control. They were two strides out from the wire and Issie was suddenly convinced that the piebald wasn't going to jump. She sat down hard in the saddle and squeezed her legs, but it didn't help.

At the very last minute, instead of taking off, Fortune baulked and swerved dramatically to the left. Issie let out a shriek and lost her balance as the pony shot out from underneath her. She felt the world go into slow motion. There was a moment when she grabbed at Fortune's neck, trying to stay on, but it was too late. She was too far over and tumbling hard, right on top of the wire fence.

Shock temporarily numbed her to the pain of impact and it took a few seconds before she felt the throbbing in her ribs. She pulled up her T-shirt and saw that a fence paling must have jabbed her because there was a big red mark. It hadn't broken the skin, but it would no doubt turn into a very purple bruise. Her hand was hurting too and she realised that she must have tried to break her fall, whacking it against the wire.

"Are you all right?" Avery yelled out.

"Yeah," said Issie, "I'm fine. Nothing broken."

Fortune, meanwhile, was still standing by the jump. He hadn't run away when Issie had fallen. He seemed to know that he should just stand and wait for his rider.

Issie grabbed his reins and led the piebald over to meet Avery who was running towards her.

"Are you sure you're OK?" he asked.

Issie nodded. "My ribs hurt a bit."

Avery looked relieved. "What do you think happened there?"

"I don't know." Issie was still shaking and trying not to look upset in front of her instructor. "He just went all wrong coming into the fence and I was trying to get him back under control. We got our striding wrong and he stopped."

"Ready to try it again then?" asked Avery.

Issie couldn't believe it. "You want me to do it again?"

"Absolutely," Avery said. "You can't stop now. We're trying to school Fortune to go over any jump you confront him with. If you quit on a bad note like this then that's the message he'll be left with at the end of training. You have to get him over this jump and end on a positive note or he'll think that stopping at the fence is the right thing to do."

Issie knew Avery was right. Fortune needed to learn that the wire was nothing to be afraid of. But how could she teach him that when inside she was still utterly shaken by her fall?

"Here," Avery said, "I'll give you a leg up."

Reluctantly, Issie let Avery lift her back into the saddle.

"Take him around the whole arena at a canter," Avery instructed. "Ride him over the white gate first to get him into stride and then turn and take the wire again. And approach it slower this time."

Issie felt sick with nerves as she rode around the arena at a canter and faced up to the white gate. Fortune jumped it easily. But once again, as he came into the wire, he began to show signs of panic, lifting his head high and speeding up. At the last minute, Issie fought to get control back, pulling hard on the reins. Then she gave a last minute kick and a growl, but it didn't help. Right in front of the jump, Fortune stopped dead.

This time, Issie managed to hang on, but she was totally shaken now. What was going wrong?

"OK," Avery said, looking serious. "Come around and do that again, but now I want you to do something for me as you come in to the wire. I want you to count the strides of the canter out loud to me. Shout them out as you approach the fence."

Issie fought back the sick feelings and the voice inside her telling her to stop as they cantered one more time around the ring. Over the white gate, she prepared herself in advance, looking at the wire. She could hear Avery's voice booming out as she approached the fence. "Let go of his mouth!" Avery was shouting. "Now put your legs on! Count the canter strides! Now!"

"One! Two! Three!" Issie shouted out loud as Fortune came in to the wire and stood off it for a split second, considering whether or not to jump. At last, he put in an extra stride, then leapt inelegantly over the fence. Issie, who hadn't quite been ready for take off, found herself flying up out of the saddle and landing with a bit of a jolt on the other side. Her pulse was racing. She was overwhelmed by adrenalin, shaking and sweating, but at least they were over!

"Well done!" Avery called out. "Much better! I think that's a good note to end him on today, don't you?"

Issie nodded gratefully. She was only too keen to finish immediately. Going over that wire had been absolutely terrifying.

"You'll get the hang of it and so will he," Avery said, as they led the piebald back to the gates. "The important thing is that you stuck with it and got him over. Riders must never give in when a horse is in training," he smiled at Issie. "You know what they say – fortune favours the brave."

Right now Issie didn't feel very brave at all. If Avery had looked at her hands, he would have seen that Issie was still shaking. In fact, she didn't stop shaking until she had ridden all the way from Winterflood Farm and was back at the pony club once more.

CHAPTER 10

With the Chevalier Point dressage day approaching, Issie had a good excuse to forget about jumping for the next week and focus on learning her dressage test.

The dressage day would be Fortune's first ever show and Issie had entered him in the novice class for horses who had never competed before. The novice test wasn't complicated – just a few twenty-metre circles and lots of trot to canter transitions. Issie had run through it a few times and been surprised to find that Fortune did it quite nicely. Even though his bloodlines were made for showjumping, and his paces were a bit rough for dressage, the piebald was doing his best to please her. She could sense that Fortune was really trying his hardest as he grunted and bounced his way through their rehearsals.

As the dressage day grew closer Issie was quietly confident that the piebald would actually put in a reasonable performance.

With all the effort she was putting into Fortune, Issie hadn't had enough time to train properly with Blaze. She was worried that the mare wouldn't be ready to do the advanced test that weekend. Issie had managed to ride Blaze a few times each week since she brought her back into work, but was that enough? Issie had been thinking about withdrawing when the decision was made for her. She turned up at the paddock two days before the show to find that Blaze was lame.

Avery came immediately, took one look at the mare and confirmed Issie's diagnosis.

"It's probably a stone bruise," he said, examining Blaze's near foreleg. "I'll call the farrier straight away. That shoe will have to come off."

The farrier clipped back the nails and levered off the metal shoe, exposing a massive stone bruise which oozed pus when it was cut open.

"It's a bad one," the farrier told Issie. "I've cut away the damaged hoof, but you'll need to poultice her for a week and you won't be able to ride her for at least a fortnight."

Issie was hugely disappointed. She had struggled to get

Blaze back into work and now this! Stella, meanwhile, had changed her mind about riding Comet too. She had been planning to enter the skewbald in the advanced class. Then, a week before the show, Mrs Tarrant took her to see a prospective pony to buy. The new pony seemed perfect and the owners had let her take him for a week on trial. Now Stella was planning to ride him at the dressage day instead of Comet.

"I'm sure he's the right one. He's not another disaster like Misty," Stella insisted. In fact, this new pony seemed like the opposite of Misty in every way, and had no conformation problems. He looked utterly perfect and even had fancy breeding and a flashy name – Quantum Leap. He was a very showy pony, a glossy bay, fourteen-two hands high with swishy, elevated paces. Avery had taken one look at Quantum Leap when he first arrived at the paddock and given him the thumbs-up on the physical. Quantum Leap – or Quanty as Stella called him – was pronounced fit and sound.

Thrilled to have her own pony again, Stella had spent the week training on Quantum Leap to compete him in the novice section. Her training sessions were going so well that, even though the pony was new, she really thought she had a chance of winning on him.

"Quanty's a really lovely mover – perfect for dressage. Plus he's supposed to be an A-grade showjumper," Stella told Issie excitedly. "Best of all, he's very, very chilled out. I've never met such a calm horse."

"So you think he's the one?" Issie asked.

"I hope so!" Stella said brightly. "I've got to make up my mind by the end of the dressage day to either buy him or give him back."

"Do you think your mum will let you buy him?" Issie asked.

"It looks like it," Stella said. "I can't imagine wanting to give him back – he's so lovely. After that awful mess with Misty, I just really want things to work out this time."

It all looked good for Quantum Leap until Sunday, the day of the dressage competition. When Issie, Kate and Mrs Brown arrived at the pony-club paddocks early that morning they found Stella standing in the paddock, in floods of tears, holding on for grim life to Quanty's lead rope, trying to control a very upset and strung-out pony.

"Thank goodness you're here." Mrs Tarrant raced over to them. "Stella's been having terrible problems with Quanty. He's being really silly and she can't get him to calm down. He's in such a state!"

Far from being his usual chilled-out self, the bay pony was twitching around on the end of the lead rope as if he were a fire walker skipping over hot coals. Stella was trying to calm him down using a soothing voice and walking him around, but nothing seemed to help.

"I don't understand it," Stella sniffled. "He wasn't like this when I got him at the start of the week. He was just lovely, really gentle and sweet. Then a few days ago he began to show signs of getting a bit overexcited and now look at him! He's been going bonkers ever since I got here this morning. I have no idea what's wrong with him."

"Maybe he's been having too much hard feed and it's made him hot?" Kate suggested.

Stella shook her head. "He's on his usual diet. He's had hardly any feed."

The girls were baffled. Quantum Leap was still behaving like an utter nervous wreck, pawing the ground and refusing to stand calmly, when Avery and Aidan turned up a few minutes later in the horse truck.

"What's up with the new pony?" Aidan asked as he jumped down from the truck cab. Stella went into an explanation of Quantum Leap's strange change in behaviour. Aidan listened and asked the same question as Kate about the hard feed. He seemed as mystified as everyone else by the pony's sudden anxiety attack. Avery, however, seemed to know exactly what was going on. He narrowed his eyes suspiciously as he examined Quantum Leap, checking the horse's breathing and noting the sweat on the bay gelding's coat.

"He's all worked up over nothing," Avery agreed. He looked at Mrs Tarrant. "How long have you had him on trial?"

"Nearly a week. We're supposed to be buying him today otherwise he'll go back to his owners."

"And you say he's only been acting strung-out in the last couple of days?" Avery asked, running his hands over a quivering Quanty. The pony was sweating profusely now and refused to keep still. Avery looked as if he was considering something. Then he turned to Stella and said, "Tell me, have you noticed his poo? Is it at all unusual?"

The others thought this was an odd and rather yucky question, but Stella seemed to perk up. "Yes! It's been really runny – you know, like cow poo!"

This seemed to confirm Avery's fears. "Stella," he said, "I hate to be the one with bad news yet again, but I think you have a problem here. This horse has a markedly different personality now than he did when he turned up at the pony club a week ago. And I'm pretty sure I know why."

Avery looked awfully serious as he continued. "I think this pony has been drugged to keep him calm."

"What?" Stella couldn't believe it. "You're kidding me."

"I wish I was," Avery said shaking his head. "It's much more common than you think. People dope horses up all the time to make them seem calm so they can sell them. I'd say the symptoms you've just described to me suggest that this horse was given an injection of Reserpine. It's a drug that makes nervous horses change personality and seem more relaxed. The thing is, this drug has side-effects – like the runny poo that you've noticed. Plus it only lasts about a week. Now that the drug is wearing off, Quantum Leap is starting to reveal his true nature."

"Poor Quanty!" Stella said. She was about to step forward to give the pony a reassuring cuddle, just as she would have done with Coco, but Quantum Leap wasn't having any of it. As Stella approached him he pulled back really hard on his lead rope, snapping the baling twine that had been holding him to the fence. He would have bolted if Aidan's reflexes hadn't been lightning fast. Aidan was used to handling spooky ponies and his reactions were so quick, he'd leapt forward before anyone else could even think to move. He grabbed Quanty's lead rope and in one smooth fluid movement he was at the bay pony's side, talking softly to him.

"I'll walk him for a bit and try to calm him down," he told Mrs Tarrant and Stella, "while you decide what to do next."

Avery suggested that they could call the vet in to do a test. "It might not be doping," he pointed out, "but I'm pretty certain that I'm right – Quanty is exhibiting all the classic signs of a pony that's been drugged."

"I don't think we need to call the vet," Mrs Tarrant said firmly. Instead, she got on the phone immediately to Quantum Leap's owners and accused them point-blank of doping the pony.

Of course they denied it at first, but Mrs Tarrant pushed the point and finally Quanty's owners admitted that the pony was "inclined to tense up" and might have "occasionally" been given a shot to keep him calm.

Mrs Tarrant was appalled and let them have it for putting both the pony and her daughter at risk, telling them that they could pick up their horse straight away. Stella, meanwhile, was inconsolable. Quantum Leap wasn't her perfect pony after all. There was only an hour until the competition got under way and once more Stella was stuck without a horse. It was too late to enter Comet, and anyway there wasn't the time to get him plaited.

"You can ride Marmite if you like," Aidan kindly offered. "He's been entered and he's all ready to go. You'll have no trouble with him."

"Are you sure?" Stella said.

"Totally!" Aidan grinned at her. "I've still got Jasper to ride. Besides, I'm here to give the horses some experience before we sell them at the auction – and I can't think of a better experience for Marmite than having a change of rider. It will be good for him."

Stella gratefully accepted Aidan's offer. But that only left her an hour before the competition to get on Marmite for the very first time and build a partnership with the brown pony. And Marmite happened to be the first horse scheduled to compete in the arena when the novice classes began that morning.

Aidan gave Stella some quick advice as they warmed Marmite up, but he was holding his breath along with everyone else when Stella rode into the ring and saluted the judge to begin her test. Everyone was amazed when, despite having only been together for a very short time, Stella and Marmite put in a really polished performance.

"You're a superstar!" Stella hugged the brown pony as they left the ring. A few moments later she positively whooped with delight when she saw their score get posted on the board. Marmite had got eights for his paces and the partnership had scored brilliant marks for most of the test, especially their transitions.

Jasper, the second Blackthorn Pony to compete that morning, put in a nice test as well. Aidan was very happy with the chestnut pony, although they had a few tense moments when they broke out of a canter in the wrong spot and lost points. When the final scores for the morning were posted on the board before lunch it was Marmite in the lead, with just a handful of novice-class competitors still to come – including Issie and Fortune.

Issie was the first to go in the arena after the lunch break and so she bolted down her food and made sure she had plenty of time to warm up before she was due to be called in to do her test.

Warming up properly was important with a horse like Fortune. Issie had to make sure the piebald was really listening to her leg aids. She worked him around in a circle and asked the piebald for lots of transitions, from walk to trot to canter and back again, making sure he was paying attention. Then, five minutes before she was due to be called, she trotted him over to the arena to see if the judge was ready for her.

She could see the judge, a tiny woman called Marjory Allwell, sitting in the front seat of her car, as dressage judges often do, with the vehicle parked to face the dressage ring so that she could watch the test from the driver's seat.

As Issie trotted Fortune around the outside of the arena Marjory Allwell gave a honk on her car horn – the official signal that she was ready for the next rider to enter the ring.

Issie felt a sudden surge of nerves. Once she entered the arena, every step that they took would be judged and given points towards their total score. Fortune couldn't afford to put a foot wrong.

As they entered the arena Issie could feel Fortune tense up a little, as if he knew everyone's eyes were on him. Issie worried for a moment that the piebald pony might lose his cool. He had never competed before and often ponies found the pressure the first time was too much for them. Fortune, however, seemed to love it and was relishing the opportunity to show off.

The piebald started the test brilliantly, halting perfectly with his feet square beneath him as Issie saluted the judge. Marjory Allwell saluted back and they moved off at a trot, keeping a steady rhythm. In the next corner, Issie asked Fortune to canter and the piebald executed the move right on cue. The pony was settling into his routine nicely and Issie felt her nerves disappear as the adrenalin rush of competing took over.

She was just about to do a twenty-metre circle at M when, for no reason at all, Fortune suddenly spooked! He propped on his front feet and came to a dead stop, flinging Issie forward so that she landed hard on his neck and had to struggle her way back into the saddle.

"Fortune!" Issie squealed in shock. She managed to regain her seat, but she couldn't for the life of her understand why Fortune had suddenly done that in the middle of the test.

Then she looked up and saw that it wasn't the piebald's fault. Fortune hadn't spooked at nothing – there was a man in the dressage arena! He had appeared out of nowhere and he was striding through the middle of the ring. He must have walked straight into Fortune's eyeline as he cut ahead of the pony! No wonder the piebald had panicked and shied!

The man was dressed in a pair of bright red plus fours with a matching tam-o'-shanter and Issie recognised him immediately. It was Gordon Cheeseman.

The golf-club manager must have leapt over the rope fence of the dressage ring and he seemed totally oblivious to the fact that he was ruining Issie's test as he strode aggressively, swinging a golf club in time with his steps.

Gordon Cheeseman didn't notice or care that he had startled a horse and nearly caused an accident. Issie and Fortune were of no interest to him. He had spotted Marjory Allwell in the car, dressed in her formal navy suit and, assuming she was a person of great importance, he made a beeline for her.

"Are you the one who's in charge around here?" he bellowed at poor Marjory. "I need to talk to someone instead of that Avery idiot! Who's really running this club?"

Marjory Allwell was an experienced dressage judge, but she had never been to Chevalier Point Pony Club before today, and she had never dealt with anything like this before. Why was this ridiculous-looking man barging into the middle of the arena, yelling his head off and swinging a golf club like some kind of maniac?

The judge leapt out of her car and addressed Gordon

Cheeseman in a booming voice, much louder than you might think that a woman of her diminutive size would possess.

"Sir! Please leave the arena immediately! Can't you see there's a rider in the middle of competing and you're in the way?"

"I'll do no such thing!" Gordon Cheeseman snapped back. "You don't know who you're dealing with."

Judge Marjory was now beginning to fear for her safety. This lunatic waggling his golf club looked like he was on a short fuse and he was showing no signs of leaving. She was about to reach back into her car to honk the horn again to summon help when she saw Avery running across the paddock with Aidan close behind him.

"What's all this nonsense about, Gordon?" Avery said. "You do realise you're ruining a dressage competition by charging around like a madman?"

"Got your attention then, have I?" Gordon Cheeseman growled. "Excellent. Maybe somebody will finally do something about the outrage that I have just discovered."

"And what outrage is that?" asked Avery.

"Dung!" Gordon Cheeseman replied. "Mounds of the stuff. Horse dung in huge piles has been deposited all over the steps of my golf club and your pony club is responsible!"

"Gordon!" Avery said. "You're telling me you're here because of some horse dung?"

Gordon Cheeseman wasn't listening, he was too busy shouting. "Vandalism and juvenile delinquents, that's what it is!" he cried, his face turning as red as his plus fours. "Your rotten mob clearly think it's funny to dump horse poo on my doorstep! I arrived at the clubhouse just now to find a large wheelbarrow's worth of poo all over our grand marble stairs. I suppose you think it's a joke? Well, I'm here to tell you that they won't get away with it!"

"And what makes you think one of my riders did it?" Avery asked.

"Oh, for goodness' sake!" snapped Gordon Cheeseman. "Look around you, man! Who else has access to horse dung? Your pony brats have attacked my property! I won't stand for it!"

"Are you actually accusing my riders of deliberately dumping a load of horse dung on your club doorstep?"

"As if you didn't know!" Gordon Cheeseman fumed. "You're probably in on it with them. Well, it was a big mistake, Avery. A huge mistake. This is the final straw.

This is goodbye. When the council hears about this stunt there's no way they'll renew your lease. And unless you want me to call the police as well, I suggest you send a couple of your pony brats over straight away to clear up their mess and take that dung away."

"Gordon," Avery said, "my riders didn't do this."

"A likely story! You can deny it all you like, Avery, but the council won't believe you. This time you've gone too far! I want you out of here! You and your whole gang of hoodlums on horseback."

Gordon Cheeseman's voice was raised to fever pitch as crowds gathered around the edge of the arena. He turned to the assembled people. "You can go home now – the lot of you," he shouted. "As of right now, I'm closing this pony club down!"

CHAPTER 11

Normally, the sight of the maniacal golf-club manager storming off with his bright red trousers flapping in the breeze would have struck Issie as comical, but today as they watched him depart no one was laughing.

"Can he really do it?" Stella asked Avery. "Can he shut us down?"

"He can certainly complain to the council," Avery nodded, "but he can't shut us down, not today anyway."

"He's nuts!" said Stella. "As if we'd put poo on his steps."

"All the same," Avery said, "I think some of you had better go to the golf club right now with a wheelbarrow and cleaning gear and get rid of it."

"But it wasn't us!" Stella squeaked.

"We didn't do anything," Kate added indignantly. "So I don't see why we should have to clean that horrible man's stupid clubhouse steps."

"Don't get me wrong, I'm not suggesting for a moment that the attack on the golf club had anything to do with you girls," Avery said. "I'm only asking you because Gordon Cheeseman is clearly out of control and we can't afford to have him racing back here with the police, causing another scene and ruining the dressage day."

Stella and Kate could see Avery's point, and as much as it annoyed them to give Gordon Cheeseman the chance to gloat, they did as their instructor asked. They grabbed a wheelbarrow and a bucket and broom and set off down the gravel driveway to the golf-club grounds.

Meanwhile, Gordon's Cheeseman's rampage had left Issie's dressage test in tatters. She was relieved when Judge Marjory told her that the rules stated that she could start the test again from the point she had reached when the interruption occurred. Issie tried to restart the test, but by now Fortune was so stressed out and confused that when Issie rode him back into the ring he wasn't listening to her at all. On the first movement he managed to mess up his twenty-metre circles and even cantered on the wrong leg. Then disaster struck. As he came around the arena back to the point where he had spooked last time Fortune suddenly lost his cool completely, flipped out and took a sideways leap over the rope – jumping clear out of the ring!

Issie managed somehow to stay onboard, but jumping out of the ring meant instant elimination. The judge had no choice. She reluctantly honked the horn, disqualifying them.

"It wasn't Fortune's fault!" Issie was almost in tears when she met Aidan back at the horse truck. "Honestly, it's so frustrating. I had him going really well before that golf-club manager turned up acting like a crazy person in the middle of the arena…"

"Issie!"

Her complaints were cut short by Avery's arrival back at the truck. He had some good news. "I've managed to get Fortune a reprieve," he told them. "The judge agrees that there were circumstances beyond your control and the fright from the interruption was the reason Fortune spooked. She's willing to give you another go. But it's too late for another chance in the novice class. All the competitors have completed their test now and the class has been closed off."

"That doesn't sound like a reprieve." Issie was confused.

"I haven't finished," Avery said. "The judge has agreed to add you to the advanced class. She's going to let you go first at the front of the schedule. You can ride the advanced test."

"But I haven't learnt it!" Issie was horrified. "And Fortune isn't ready to compete at that level."

"I'm not saying you'll win the class," Avery conceded, "but it would be good for Fortune to have a positive experience in the arena. Horses remember things and we don't want him having a bad memory of his first dressage day. It could scar him emotionally and he'll be jumping out of the arena every time he competes."

Issie knew this was true. As for learning the test, Aidan promised to be her caller – the person who stands beside the dressage ring and yells out to the rider, telling them what movement comes next.

There was just enough time before Issie's turn for Aidan to do a practice run-through with her and then, before she knew what was happening, Issie was riding Fortune back into the ring for the third time that day, this time to do an advanced test!

From the sideline, Aidan's voice rang clear as a bell, "Enter at A – proceed, halt and salute at X" as Issie and

Fortune entered and saluted the judge.

"Proceed to C at a trot, turn left and canter at H!" Aidan shouted. Issie and Fortune struck off perfectly on his cues, turning left where the letter C was painted on to a block, going neatly into a canter when they reached the painted letter H.

"Canter down the arena and trot at K…" Aidan called out.

Again, Issie and Fortune followed his instructions perfectly. The piebald was riding brilliantly. There was a moment when they had reached the "black spot" and Issie thought Fortune might try to jump out of the ring again. She kept her hands firm and her legs on and rode Fortune forward really positively and this time the piebald didn't spook at all. After that it was plain sailing as Fortune did a brilliant test. Issie rode out of the ring as if she was floating on a cloud. She was thrilled.

Meanwhile, in the judge's car, Marjory Allwell was still recovering from her run-in with the dreadful Gordon Cheeseman. Honestly, what was wrong with people these days? Didn't they know that there were rules? Marjory Allwell, though, was in for another shock. It turned out that someone else didn't know the rules, particularly the one that stated that no one was allowed to talk to dressage judges while they were working.

Marjory was sitting in her car, with her assistant in the passenger seat next to her. The piebald pony had just finished and Marjory had honked her horn to let the next competitor know that they could enter the ring, when suddenly, the back door of the car swung open and a man jumped into the rear passenger seat so that he was sitting right behind her.

"Mind if I join you?" he said.

"Actually," replied Judge Marjory, "the next competitor is just about to enter the arena and this is most inappropriate…"

"Oh right, of course," Oliver Tucker said, totally ignoring her and thrusting his hand across the seats for Marjory to shake. "I'm Oliver Tucker, Chevalier Point Pony Club president."

"Well, it's nice to meet you, Mr Tucker," Judge Marjory said in a reserved tone. She didn't take his hand and made it quite clear that she wanted him to leave. "I'm afraid this is not a good time…"

Morgan Chatswood-Smith on Black Jack had now entered the arena and Marjory was doing her best to concentrate as Morgan gave her a salute.

"Hey, your judge-ness!" Oliver Tucker leant over her

shoulder. "What do you think? Awful legs on that one, eh?" He pointed at Black Jack. "Horrible bandy creature and a bit knock-kneed to boot, don't you think?"

"Mr Tucker!" Judge Marjory said. Hadn't she been quite firm enough? Why wouldn't this man leave?

She considered honking her car horn and stopping the rider in the ring while she called for help, but there had already been enough delays and upsets for one day. She was beginning to wish she had never come to Chevalier Point as a guest judge. The man in the back seat clearly didn't have a clue what he was talking about! Bandy? Knock-kneed? They weren't even equestrian terms! What's more, he was the club president! Surely he must realise that it was strictly against the rules to talk to the judge when she was working?

"Now there's a stunning specimen!" Oliver Tucker continued, pointing out his own daughter who was warming up on Romeo. "That's a Selle Francais that horse – beautiful animal, don't you think? I'm sure you'll want him to win the competition. There might even be a little something extra in your pay cheque if you gave him a good score…"

The judge looked at Oliver Tucker in horror. "Mr Tucker! I'm trying to work here – I don't have time to look at other horses, and if I didn't know better, I'd say you were trying to bribe me. If you are, I need to tell you that the pony-club association takes this sort of matter very seriously!"

Oliver Tucker smiled his shark-like grin. "Not at all, your judge-ness. I wasn't trying to do anything like that. I'm just giving you a tip-off, helping you out."

"Well," Marjory Allwell said coolly, "I would prefer it if you stopped helping me, thank you, Mr Tucker. In fact, I would prefer it if you would stop speaking to me altogether. I'm going to have to insist that you get out of my car!"

"Of course, of course!" Mr Tucker gave her a wink. "You're right. It's best if we're not seen together like this. We wouldn't want people to know we've made a deal, would we?"

"That wasn't what I meant at all!" said Judge Marjory. But Mr Tucker had already departed, leaving her gasping like a goldfish at his outrageous behaviour.

Ironically for Oliver Tucker, he needn't have bothered to try and bribe the judge because Natasha and Romeo put in the best test of the day anyway. Poor Marjory Allwell was frightfully embarrassed when the prize-giving was held in the clubroom at the end of the day, and she had to hand Natasha the red rosette with Oliver Tucker at the front of the crowd making a big display of winking at her.

"Your daughter won the competition fair and square, Mr Tucker," Judge Marjory said loudly.

"Of course she did!" Oliver Tucker grinned. "Say no more, Marjory!"

Morgan had won the second place rosette, Dan Halliday was third on Madonna, and Issie was thrilled when the judge announced her as the fourth best score of the day and handed her an apricot-coloured rosette. Issie wasn't worried about losing to Natasha, Morgan and Dan. They had all done excellent tests and really, considering the drama with Gordon Cheeseman and the fact that this was Fortune's first-ever advanced test, the piebald's performance had been incredible.

Gordon Cheeseman's hissy fit had turned out to be something of a blessing in disguise. Issie would never have dreamt of riding Fortune in an advanced test, but now that she had done so, she realised that the piebald was capable of much more than she had imagined.

Issie cast a glance across the clubroom to the cabinet where the Natasha Tucker Memorial Trophy sat gleaming. Maybe she did stand a chance of winning it.

Fortune was going so brilliantly, after today's dressage test she was confident the piebald could be ready to compete. The Open Gymkhana was still nearly a month away and today's performance had renewed her faith. It was time to get training...

"Admiring my trophy?" Natasha's snide remark rocked Issie back to reality. She turned around to see the snooty blonde standing right beside her.

"Enjoy looking at it while you can," continued Natasha, "because unless you pull your socks up it'll be going home with me."

"You haven't won it yet, Natasha," Issie said.

Natasha rolled her eyes. "Yeah, *whatever*, Isadora! Don't you think it's time for you to come to terms with the fact that things have changed around here? You're still riding your scruffy ponies and I'm on a proper sport-horse. When are you going to realise you're just not in my league?"

And with that, Natasha turned on her heel and headed out of the clubroom. Issie watched her leave, and at that moment a sense of determination swept over her. Suddenly, she wanted to win the trophy very badly. More than that, she wanted to make sure that Stuck-up Tucker had her comeuppance once and for all. Fortune would be ready in time for the Open Gymkhana, Issie would make sure of that. They were going to give Natasha a run for her money.

CHAPTER 12

Issie was exhausted when she arrived home after the dressage day. Mrs Brown decided that it was too late in the evening to cook dinner and bought them takeaway fish and chips as a treat. "Why don't you have a bath and get an early night?" her mother suggested. "You got up at six so you must be tired, and you've got school in the morning."

The mention of school made Issie panic. Upstairs in her bedroom two weeks' worth of homework was sitting on her desk, still unfinished.

The last thing Issie felt like was hitting the books, but tonight was her last chance. Two of the assignments were due in tomorrow and she had to get them done. If her mum found out that Issie was slipping behind on her homework, she'd be bound to blame her riding. And so Issie readily agreed to the suggestion of an early night, and sat down at her study desk to try and do a fortnight's worth of work in one evening.

By 10 p.m. she was slumped over her maths book, unable to go on any longer. At times like these, she decided, there was only one thing for it. She needed chocolate. She had seen a bar of fruit and nut in the fridge earlier – that would give her some brain energy for sure.

Issie crept downstairs. Her mum had already gone to bed and the downstairs lights were out. She didn't bother to turn them on as she padded in her socks across the kitchen.

The moon was three-quarters full outside and its light flooded in through the French doors. Issie tiptoed her way across the floor to the fridge, trying to tread softly so she wouldn't wake her mum. She swung open the door and the fridge light illuminated her face as she peered inside. Where had her mum hidden that chocolate? Finally, Issie found it underneath the lettuce – her mum obviously thought the vegetable compartment was the one place her daughter would never look for food!

Issie was unwrapping the foil from the chocolate bar

when she suddenly had the sensation that she was being watched. Spinning around to the French doors, she stared out and saw a face at the window. The sight nearly made her leap out of her skin.

"Ohmygod!"

Two eyes were looking at her through the glass. But they weren't human eyes. They were coal black, staring out from a snowy white face.

"Mystic!" Issie hissed. "You scared me half to death!"

She ran over to the French doors, quickly worked the lock open and stepped outside on to the patio. Mystic, who was waiting for her, nickered softly.

"Shush!" Issie whispered. "Mum might still be awake."

She looked at the grey pony. What was he doing here? Did he have to be here tonight of all nights? She was way behind on her homework and she really needed to get it done. Now it looked like that was never going to happen. Whatever the reason was for Mystic's appearance, it was obviously more important than homework.

"Stay here," she told him. "I'm going to get my boots on. I'll be quick."

Issie sprinted lightly back upstairs to her room, grabbed her jodhpur boots and her polar fleece, then hurried straight back downstairs again. Outside on the back lawn she yanked on the fleece and boots as fast as she could and then she followed Mystic, who was already heading through the garden towards the gate that led out to the road.

It was a bitterly cold night and Issie was glad she had bothered to grab some warm clothes. As she put out her hand to touch Mystic's soft dapple-grey coat she could sense the warmth of her pony, and yet she still felt a chill up her spine at the same time. Mystic's appearance always meant that something dark and dangerous was afoot. Why was the grey pony here this time?

There was no time to worry about that now. Mystic was anxious to go and as soon as Issie opened the gate he dashed through to the other side. Issie climbed the rungs and then took a graceful, catlike leap, landing neatly on his back.

Mystic headed down the back streets behind Issie's house, taking the same route they had followed just a few weeks ago when they had ridden to the pony club and found the fence cut open and Fortune on the golf course.

As the streetlights lit the way above them Issie stared up at the dark, cloudy sky and wondered what lay ahead. Blaze, Comet and Fortune were all at the pony-club paddocks – so was Kate's horse Toby. Was one of them in danger?

She became even more nervous when Mystic reached the main road and turned to the left once more. There was no doubt in Issie's mind now that the grey gelding was taking her to the pony club. She was sure it had something to do with the horses and she only hoped they would be in time to save them.

As Mystic began to gallop along the verge beside the main road Issie gripped with her knees and clung on to his long, ropey mane, as the grey pony sped on. The main road to the club grounds wasn't far to ride at a gallop, but tonight it seemed to take an eternity. Issie was trying to keep calm, trying not to think of the worst as Mystic turned the corner from the main road and took the gravel driveway that led to the pony-club entrance.

Then something strange happened. Issie had been expecting the pony to pull up to a halt at the gates, but instead, Mystic kept galloping. He ran on past them, still at a gallop, his strides never slowing.

"Mystic!" Issie shouted, her voice catching in the wind. "Stop! You're going the wrong way."

She pulled at his mane, trying to get him to change course, but it was no good. Mystic was ignoring her protests and galloping on. They were further down the driveway now, far away from the streetlights of the main road. With no lamp posts, all she had was moonlight to help her see. Issie tried to peer into the inky blackness ahead, but the wind was against her face now and it was cold enough to make her eyes water. She lifted one hand to wipe her eyes, still gripping Mystic's mane tightly with her other hand.

All around her, on both sides of the road, the black shapes of trees towered over her, blocking out the moonlight so that she could barely see more than a horse length or two ahead. Issie had no idea where they were going. It wasn't until Mystic rounded a corner that she could finally see a light glowing softly about a hundred metres ahead of them.

The driveway led to the golf club and Issie realised that the light must be coming from the clubhouse. As she got closer she could see it more clearly. The lights were on in a room on the lower floor, their yellow glow illuminating the grand bay windows.

In fact, the whole building was grand, built in the ostentatious style of an old Georgian manor house. It was constructed from bright red brick, with cream trim around the doors and windows. A large colonnade with marble pillars and matching steps led up to the front of the building from the driveway. It must have been here that the horse manure was dumped earlier that day – the dung having since been cleared up by Stella and Kate.

The marble steps led to an enormous front door. Golf-club members entered through this front door and then either proceeded up a vast marble staircase to the first floor or continued on the ground-floor level. On the corner of the ground floor, overlooking both the lawn and the gravel driveway, was a meeting room. It was in this room that the lights now blazed and, right outside, two cars were parked in the parking bays by the turning circle at the end of the driveway. Issie saw the cars and realised that the clubhouse lights hadn't been left on by mistake. It was almost midnight and yet there were definitely people still here.

Issie spoke softly to Mystic, using her voice to slow the grey gelding down to a trot, veering off the gravel driveway and on to the lawn that bordered the end of the driveway and flowed down into the golf course beyond. Mystic's hoofbeats, which had been making a clean chime against the hard gravel, were now muffled and quiet as they struck against the soft surface of the grass. Whoever was inside the clubhouse wouldn't hear them coming.

But why would anyone be here on a Sunday night at this hour? The bar and the restaurant were both closed, and no one would be playing a round of golf in the middle of the night.

On the grass, just a few metres away from the bay windows, Issie slid off the grey pony's back and landed lightly on the ground. She dropped low and stayed crouched down, creeping forward like an army commando until she was beneath the windows of the meeting room and hidden from view. She pressed her back up against the cool, red bricks of the clubhouse wall, as still as a statue, listening to her own breathing coming fast and shallow, her heart racing.

Issie was dying to know who was inside, but she had to be careful and make sure she couldn't be seen. She could hear voices – male voices. Very slowly, she raised her head and peered in through the window.

Two men were sitting at the table. One of them was Gordon Cheeseman and sitting opposite him, with his back to the window, was another man. Issie couldn't see who he was at first, but then a moment later, he turned around and Issie recognised the sharp features of Oliver

Tucker. She was still staring when suddenly, Oliver Tucker looked towards the windows straight at her! Issie panicked and ducked down, hoping that she hadn't been seen. She held her breath as she heard Oliver Tucker stand up from his chair... but it was OK. He hadn't seen her. He was only standing up so that he could unroll a large tube of paper on to the table.

"These are the plans," he said to Gordon Cheeseman.

The golf-club manager leant over the table and examined the blueprints. He made admiring noises. "It looks superb, Oliver," he said. "Another first-class property development. You've really outdone yourself this time."

"I'm glad you think so, Gordon," said Oliver Tucker, "because you're the first one to see it. I knew you'd be thrilled. I'm going to build a luxury country-club complex right next to your golf course. I knew immediately that you would see how this could benefit us both because you're a man of great vision, much like myself."

Gordon Cheeseman looked pleased and extremely flattered – exactly as Oliver Tucker had intended.

"The thing is, Gordon," he continued, "a golf course like yours needs the right sort of neighbours. When we get rid of the pony club and I build my luxury country-club apartments on the same spot there'll be no more riff-raff bothering you. You'll have a whole host of wealthy golfers living next door instead. Your business will boom!"

"That does sound wonderful," agreed Gordon Cheeseman.

"Indeed." Oliver Tucker was now ready to go in for the kill. "I think we're in agreement. All I need is your signature on a few forms that I have to lodge with the council. Just a bit of paperwork to say you approve of my application as your new neighbour. Then, once this is done, I'll meet with my financial backers, get them to sign the paperwork and it's official."

Gordon Cheeseman smiled. "I must say this is a stroke of good fortune for the golf club," he said, leaning over the blueprints once more. "Just when I've come to the end of my tether with that dreadful pony club, you turn up with a plan for a development of upmarket apartments right on the land where the pony club sits! It's brilliant, Oliver, and jolly good timing as far as I'm concerned. I'll be happy to see the back of those kids and their grubby ponies."

"Well." Oliver Tucker smoothed back his blond hair,

"you'll have no problems there. After all, I'm the club president. I've already arranged for the club to give up their lease and move to the River Paddock. And with horses escaping on to the golf course and those rider-vandals dumping muck on your steps, there's no way the council will block the move."

Gordon Cheeseman shook his head. "I wish I'd caught those kids in the act, dumping horse poo at my club! I'm sure they were responsible – little hooligans."

"Of course they were," Oliver Tucker said, smooth as silk. "Anyway, as I was saying, all I need is your signature here, here and here."

He handed over a piece of paper which Gordon Cheeseman duly signed and initialled.

"Congratulations, Gordon." Oliver Tucker shook his hand. "You're about to get rid of that pony club and get yourself some lovely, rich new neighbours."

"Excellent!" Gordon Cheeseman said. "Shall we have a wee dram of whisky to celebrate?" He strode over towards the drinks cabinet, which was positioned by the window and Issie had to duck down fast once more. As she crouched low beneath the window frame she could see his shadow standing above her and hear the sound of glasses clinking and rattling.

"Would you like ice with yours, Ollie? I've got some here somewhere…" he began to say. Then he stopped.

"What the blazes was that?"

Mystic, who had been standing quietly in the shadows on the lawn, waiting for Issie, had suddenly got impatient and had given a loud nicker.

"Did you hear it?" Gordon Cheeseman put down the whisky bottle and stared out the window.

"Hear what?" Oliver Tucker came over to join him. Crouched down outside the window, Issie could feel the presence of the two men above her. Her heart was pounding like mad.

There was silence as they stared out into the darkness. Gordon Cheeseman put down the whisky bottle. "I think I'd better take a look outside," he said. "If those pony-club vandals are back then they'll soon discover that Gordon Cheeseman is not a man you want to mess with!"

Beneath the window, Issie froze in horror like a deer caught in the headlights. What should she do? Gordon Cheeseman was bound to see her – and then what?

Blind panic took over as she looked around. Mystic was on the lawn about twenty metres away from her, pacing restlessly. Should she make a dash for him right now? It was risky – what if she wasn't quick enough and the two men saw her? But if she stayed where she was then Gordon Cheeseman would spot her for sure and she would definitely be caught.

For a split second, Issie was riveted to the spot, terrified and gripped by indecision. Then Mystic nickered again, much louder this time, as if he was trying to make her mind up for her. *Run to me!* Mystic seemed to be saying. *It's your only chance! Come now!*

Issie suddenly realised that Mystic was right. She had no choice. As footsteps echoed up the hall she knew she was out of time. With her heart racing and her blood pounding she leapt to her feet and ran.

CHAPTER 13

Issie sprinted across the lawn. She was so scared her legs felt like rubber, quivering beneath her. She knew the men wouldn't be far behind. It would only take them a minute, maybe less, to walk the length of the clubhouse hallway to the front door. She and Mystic had to get out of here before Gordon Cheeseman and Oliver Tucker had the chance to open it.

As she approached the grey pony she realised there was no time to find a mounting block. Instead, she decided to do something she had never done before. In desperation, she kept running as fast as she could. She didn't slow down as she got closer; instead, she paced her strides and swung her arms like a gymnast approaching a vaulting horse. She was about a metre away from Mystic when she suddenly flung herself into the air, grabbing at his mane with both hands, hauling herself up on to his back.

She leapt with such force that she managed to get her right leg up and over Mystic's rump. Now, straining with both arms, she pulled herself up so that she was on his back. She had done it! She had vaulted on! Mystic tried to keep still while Issie scrambled her way up until she was safely on and ready to go.

But where were they going to go? Gordon Cheeseman would be stepping outside any moment now, and if Issie cantered back up the driveway, she would have to ride right past the front door of the clubhouse. Her only choice was to turn Mystic in the opposite direction and ride him across the golf-club grounds!

"C'mon," she clucked the grey pony on, "let's go."

Issie could see a small grove of conifer trees just beyond the first tee and she headed straight for them, leaning low over Mystic's wither and urging him into a gallop. They made it to the trees just in time. If Gordon Cheeseman had looked in that direction as he came out on to the steps of the clubhouse, he might just have caught a glimpse of Mystic's silvery tail as he slipped behind the trees. But by the time he did look their way, Issie and Mystic disappeared.

"Do you see anything?" Oliver Tucker came out on to the steps to join Gordon Cheeseman who was straining his eyes, staring into the blackness.

"No." The golf-club manager shook his head. "There's no one there. Must have been a horse over at the pony club – the sound really travels around here at night."

"Right!" said Oliver Tucker looking at his watch, clearly losing interest in the whole matter. "Anyway, it's late. I'd better be going." He held the blueprints of his luxury apartments rolled up in one hand and he extended the other for Gordon Cheeseman to shake. "We'll have those drinks another time if you don't mind, Gordon."

"What? Oh, yes, of course..." Gordon Cheeseman was still staring distractedly out into the night. "It's so queer though. I could have sworn I heard a horse right outside the window."

"Pleasure doing business with you, Gordon," said Oliver Tucker as he climbed into his Ferrari and threw the blueprints on to the passenger seat. "Let's have that drink next month on the fifteenth, shall we? That's the date that I'm meeting my financiers here at the golf club to sign off on the deal."

"Top stuff!" Gordon Cheeseman said, waving goodbye. "See you then."

Issie stayed behind the trees as they said their farewells. She didn't move a muscle as she watched the golf-club manager go back inside and switch off the lights, then lock the front door and get into his own car. It wasn't until well after Gordon Cheeseman had driven off into the night that she finally emerged from behind the conifers, still shaking with the shock of her narrow escape. She waited another few minutes until she was certain that the men had really gone and weren't coming back before she rode Mystic out again to head home.

"Well done, Mystic." She patted the grey pony beneath her. "You saved me back there, boy."

Now that she knew what was going on, Issie couldn't believe that she had actually doubted Mystic when he had refused to turn in at the pony club. She didn't realise what his real mission was and she had been looking for trouble in the wrong place. But the truth they'd uncovered tonight was much worse than she could have ever imagined.

"Oh, Mystic," she breathed softly to her pony. "What are we going to do?"

It was clear to her now, even if it wasn't obvious to that fool Gordon Cheeseman, that Oliver Tucker was behind the vandalism. He was the one who had cut the fence, and he was the one who had dumped dung on the golf-club steps. The property developer was deliberately sabotaging Chevalier Point Pony Club, determined to get his hands on its land for his own selfish, money-grubbing purposes. Gordon Cheeseman was just a puppet in his game, and the golf-club manager was too vain to realise it. The only ones who knew the truth right now were Issie and Mystic. And they couldn't stop Oliver Tucker alone.

Issie's first thought was that she should tell her mum what Natasha's dad was planning. But on the ride home she discounted that notion pretty quickly. Ever since she had got back from Spain her mum had been worrying about her. If she knew that Issie had skipped doing her homework and had ridden down the main road to the pony club by herself at night, Issie would never hear the end of it. But how else could she explain overhearing the conversation between the two men? That ruled out telling Avery too. He would be duty-bound to tell her mother – which just led to exactly the same problem.

Issie still didn't know what to do when she woke up the next morning and so she didn't say anything at breakfast. Instead, she wolfed down her toast and biked off to school. It was Monday and that meant Stella and Kate would both be in her first class at nine. That would give her the chance to tell her friends what she'd found out.

Well, not the whole story of course – they didn't know about Mystic. But Issie just told them that she'd biked up to the club to check on the horses, happened to notice the lights on at the golf club and had gone to check it out. Stella and Kate didn't question this at all – they were too busy being totally gobsmacked by the news that Mr Tucker was trying to sabotage the pony club.

"You mean he convinced everyone that we needed to move to the River Paddock just so he could take over the lease on the land and build some luxury development?" Kate shook her head in disbelief.

"Exactly!" Issie said. "Remember that first rally day when he started up about the golf balls and how unsafe the club grounds are? I'm sure he planted those balls himself.

And that night we saw him with the measuring wheel? He must have been pacing out where the apartments would be built. And I'm positive that he cut the fence and dumped the dung on Gordon Cheeseman's steps. He's been playing us off against the golf club, trying to convince them that we're bad neighbours. He's made sure Gordon Cheeseman will support him in case there's any reluctance from the club members when we quit the lease next month."

"But why would he do all this? What's in it for him?" Stella said.

"Oh, duh, Stella!" said Kate. "Money of course! Oliver Tucker is a property developer. He makes his cash from building apartments – and the pony club is on prime land right next to a luxury golf course. We've been there so long, no one's noticed that land must be worth a bomb in today's market."

Issie nodded. "It must have been Mr Tucker's plan all along when he became president. Why else would he suddenly be interested in Natasha and her horses?"

"So what do we do now?" asked Kate.

"We call the police!" Stella said. "Issie, you have to tell them everything."

"Tell them what?" said Issie. "Property development

isn't a crime. If the pony club chooses not to renew that lease, there's nothing illegal about Mr Tucker making a bid for it. And we can't prove any of the stuff about the fence cutting and horse dung."

"So he's going to get away with it?" Stella couldn't believe her ears.

"No," Issie said. "I didn't say that. If we can convince the pony-club committee to throw out his plans and refuse to move the club then there's nothing he can do."

"But remember," Issie continued, "Mr Tucker is really good at talking his way out of stuff. Plus he's the adult – so they'll never believe us if we don't have proof."

"So what do we do then?" asked Stella.

"We get our hands on the plans," Issie said. "The ones that I saw him show Mr Cheeseman. If the club committee saw those blueprints then they'd know that Oliver Tucker has been intending to take over the land and make money from it right from the start."

"So how do we get our hands on them?"

Issie shook her head. "I don't know,' she admitted. "All I know is that Mr Tucker's having his big meeting with his financial backers at the golf course next month to seal the deal."

"Then we need to figure out a way to get our hands

on the blueprints before then," Stella said.

"Yeah, right." Kate rolled her eyes. "What are we going to do? Break into his safe? Who are you, Kim Possible?"

Stella shot her a sulky look. "I just want to save the pony club."

"We all want to save the pony club," Issie said, "and we'll think of something."

"We'll meet up after school," said Stella. "We can talk about it then."

Aidan picked Issie and the others up after school and she told him the whole story as they drove to the pony club.

"We need those blueprints as proof," Aidan said. "Are you sure Mr Tucker didn't leave them at the golf club?"

Issie shook her head. "I saw him put them in his Ferrari."

"Maybe they're still in the car?" Stella said. "He probably keeps them with him for meetings."

"We need to get a look inside that Ferrari and find out," Aidan agreed.

"The next rally day is two weeks away," said Issie. "It'll have to be then."

"And what do we do now?" Stella asked.

"We wait and we keep our eyes open. Mr Tucker is bound to try some more sabotage," said Kate.

Issie disagreed. "I don't think he'll do anything else. He's already convinced the pony-club parents that the club grounds are unsafe, and now he's got Gordon Cheeseman to sign his papers too. He doesn't need to pull any more stunts. He'll probably lay low until his meeting on the fifteenth with his financial backers."

"The fifteenth?" Kate said.

"Yeah. That was the date he told Gordon Cheeseman. That's when the deal is going to happen. Why?"

"There's something about that date that sounds very familiar," said Kate.

"It should sound familiar," Stella replied. "It's been in my diary for months."

Everyone looked blank.

"Don't you remember?" Stella was exasperated. "The fifteenth is the Open Gymkhana – the day we're competing for the Tucker Trophy!"

CHAPTER 14

For the first time ever at a pony-club rally, Issie was actually pleased to see Natasha Tucker. Well, not exactly pleased, but she had been worried that Natasha wouldn't come today. It was the last club day before the gymkhana and that meant it was their last chance to get their hands on Mr Tucker's blueprints.

As the Tuckers' silver and blue horse truck drove in through the gates, Issie's sense of relief was short-lived. "The blueprints won't be in the horse truck," Stella pointed out. "Mr Tucker put them in his car."

"Look!" Kate said, pointing over at the red Ferrari that had just driven up beside the truck. "Nothing to worry about. He's here as well!"

As Mrs Tucker helped Natasha unload her horse

from the truck Mr Tucker, dressed in a suit as usual and wearing sunglasses pushed up on top of his head, made calls on his mobile phone. He was striding about as he spoke, his voice booming across the pony-club paddocks as he barked orders at whoever was on the other end of the line. Oliver Tucker continued talking on the phone as he strode off towards the clubroom.

"Do you think the blueprints are still in the car?" Stella asked.

"Only one way to find out," said Issie. She gave her two friends a grin over her shoulder as she mounted up on Fortune. "Wish me luck!"

Being on horseback worked to Issie's advantage. As she came closer to the red Ferrari she had a good view into the convertible. She tried to look casual as she rode right up and peered into the passenger seat. There was nothing there. Perhaps the plans were in the boot?

Issie slid down off Fortune and put one hand on the boot of the Ferrari. She tried to find the push-button lock, but she couldn't see it anywhere. She was puzzling over this when a voice right beside her startled her.

"What are you doing?" Natasha Tucker asked icily.

"Ummm, I was just looking at the car," Issie said.

"Well, I wouldn't get too close if I were you," Natasha

said. "Daddy's very protective of his Ferrari."

"Yeah, it's pretty amazing," Issie said.

"He used to drive a Lamborghini," said Natasha airily, "but he likes the Ferrari better." She had a cruel smile on her face as she added casually, "What sort of car does your father drive?"

"My dad?" Issie said.

"Yes. I don't think I've ever seen him here at the pony club, have I?"

Issie looked at the smug expression on Natasha's face. The snooty blonde knew only too well that Issie's mum and dad had split up a long time ago and Mr Brown was no longer around. He had moved out and left Chevalier Point when Issie was nine and she had hardly seen him since. Issie was OK about it. She'd got used to the fact that her dad wasn't there. Even so, her friends all knew better than to bring it up. But then Natasha wasn't a friend, was she?

As Natasha stood there smirking something in Issie snapped. At least Issie's dad wasn't trying to do dodgy property deals that would ruin the Chevalier Point Pony Club! Did Natasha even know what her father was really up to? "Your dad's been here a lot lately, hasn't he?" Issie shot back.

Natasha stiffened. "Well, he is the club president."

"Yes, he is, isn't he?" said Issie. "Which is kind of strange, don't you think, since he never, ever turned up to watch you ride before, and now suddenly he's here all the time."

Natasha glared back at Issie. "My dad's a very busy man."

"Oh, I know," said Issie. "He's busy with midnight meetings and secret business deals to make money by destroying the pony club!"

"What are you on about?" Natasha looked upset. "My dad is a property developer. He doesn't do secret deals."

"So he's told you all about his plan to get rid of the pony club and build luxury, country-club apartments?" Issie asked.

Natasha, for once, was dumbstruck.

"So he hasn't told you?" said Issie. "Well, why don't you ask him? He's—" Issie was about to continue when suddenly, Mr Tucker arrived back from the clubroom.

Oliver Tucker looked at Issie standing there holding Fortune's reins. "Hello there, are you a friend of Natasha's?" he asked.

"Not really," Issie said without thinking.

"Dad?" Natasha looked upset. "Isadora's been saying

things about you getting rid of the pony club so that you can build apartments here!"

The smile suddenly disappeared from Oliver Tucker's face. He swung around to face Issie, and his eyes turned cold and black.

"Now, Isadora," he said through clenched teeth, the words coming out with deliberate care. "Where on earth would you hear a rumour like that?"

"Ummm…" Issie was getting nervous. She looked around. "I don't remember…"

Mr Tucker took a deep breath and forced a shark-like smile back on to his face once more.

"I don't know what you've been hearing, young lady," he said in a patronising tone as if he were talking to a five-year-old, "but you've got the wrong end of the stick. Business deals are very complicated and you probably wouldn't understand, but anything I'm doing will only be for the very best. Remember, it's not me who wants to move the pony club to the River Paddock – the committee makes the final decision. I'm just doing their bidding!"

Mr Tucker grinned at her again and Issie felt herself subconsciously stepping back to get away from him.

"I'd better get going," Issie said. "The rally is about to start."

"Nice to meet you, Isadora," Oliver Tucker said. "A word of warning though. Be careful about repeating rumours like that one. You wouldn't want to end up in trouble by saying the wrong thing now, would you?"

As he said this the charming smile slipped a bit again, and Issie caught a glimpse of the real Oliver Tucker, all steely and menacing. Was he threatening her? She wasn't sure, but suddenly Issie desperately wanted to get away from him.

She stumbled backwards and yanked on Fortune's reins so hard that the piebald almost leapt on top of her as she wheeled him around. "See you later," she managed to stammer. As she walked her pony away she could feel Oliver Tucker's eyes boring holes in her back. Her heart was beating like a drum as she led Fortune back to Avery's horse truck to rejoin the others.

Two facts had suddenly become crystal clear. The first was that Oliver Tucker was now wise to the fact that Issie knew about his plan. That meant she would have to be super-careful from now on – he would be watching her. The second thing was that Natasha Tucker knew absolutely nothing about her father's schemes. She couldn't possibly have been faking that shocked expression when Issie told her about the secret meeting

– she wasn't a good enough actress.

"Well, we know what's really going on," Stella said when Issie met them back at the truck, "but we still have no proof."

"Are you sure the blueprints weren't in the car?" asked Kate.

"Not entirely," Issie admitted. "I tried to open the boot to have a look, but there was no handle!"

"Oh, you didn't!" Aidan rolled his eyes at her. "Issie, Ferraris don't have boots – the engine is in the back!"

Issie felt silly. "No wonder there wasn't a handle."

"Well, what's in the front if the engine is in the back?" Stella asked.

"There's usually some storage space up front under the bonnet," said Aidan.

"So maybe he keeps the blueprints in there?" Kate suggested.

"Too late to look now," Issie sighed. "Natasha knows something is up and besides, the rally is about to start."

"You guys go and ride, and leave the blueprints to me," Aidan said confidently.

Everyone turned to stare at him. "Why you?" Stella pouted.

"Come on!" Aidan reasoned. "I've got a better chance than the rest of you. Natasha doesn't have the knives out for me – she barely knows who I am." They all agreed that this was true.

"Meanwhile," Issie said, "we're supposed to be focusing on training to win that Tucker Trophy."

Issie looked serious. "I can't stand the thought of losing the pony-club grounds and the trophy to Natasha as well!"

"Whoa, Issie!" Kate said with a grin. "Priority check! What's more important? The future of the pony club or taking home some silly trophy?"

Issie knew that Kate had a point. Now they knew Oliver Tucker's real purpose here at the pony club, the Tucker Trophy shouldn't have mattered to them any more. Yet she couldn't help it. Stuck-up Tucker had already been so obnoxious about the trophy, Issie couldn't bear the idea of her gloating for a whole year. There was no way she was going to let that bratty blonde take the golden horse home without a fight.

Natasha certainly looked like the hot favourite to win the trophy. Romeo was such a beautiful horse with incredibly floaty paces; he stood out from the rest as they rode their workout that morning. The rally day had flown by without mishap and before they knew it, Avery was asking his senior riders to line up next to the Open Hunter course for the end of the day's lesson.

"Since this is our last training session before the gymkhana," he told them, "I thought I'd give you the chance to let me know what you want to do. Is there anything that you really need to practise? Do any of you have a 'bogey fence', a jump that's giving you problems?" Issie glanced over at the wire jump. She hadn't had the guts to try it again since that day with Avery and looking at the jump now she felt her heart thumping hard in her chest, her breath quickening. "Issie?" Avery said. "Do you have a jump you'd like to have one more go at?"

She knew at that moment that she should tell Avery. But the idea of jumping the wire made her feel sick. She couldn't face the thought of failing all over again in front of everyone.

"No," Issie lied, "I'm not having any problems."

Avery looked intently at her. "OK then. If there's nothing else anyone wants to work on, let's finish up for the day. You can all go back to your horse trucks and untack."

Back at the horse truck the girls had untacked and rugged the ponies up ready to leave when they noticed that Aidan wasn't there.

"Where is he?" Stella sighed. "I want to go."

Aidan, as it turned out, was where he'd told the others he would be. He was making one final bid to get his hands on the blueprints.

As the riders headed back to their trucks he'd walked straight up to Natasha and started chatting. Aidan told her that he was very interested in sports cars and then asked her very nicely if she would show him the Ferrari. Natasha had been surprisingly keen on the idea and by the time Issie and the others spotted him, Aidan was actually sitting in the front seat with Natasha in the passenger seat next to him.

"What is he doing?" Stella was amazed.

"Never mind him!" Issie snapped. "What is she doing?"

Natasha was behaving in a most un-Natasha-like manner. She was gazing intently at Aidan and twiddling with her blonde plaits. There was something very weird about her. Issie couldn't put her finger on it at first, and then she realised what it was. Natasha was smiling. Not just a bit – she was giggling and hanging off Aidan's every word as if he was saying the most hilarious things she had ever heard. Issie watched as Aidan said something else to Natasha and she burst into giggles again.

Then Natasha pressed a button on the dashboard and the bonnet popped open. They both promptly got out of the car and Natasha helped Aidan to open the bonnet and look inside. Then Aidan slammed it shut again and there was some more unbearably flirty plait-twiddling and silly giggling before he finally said goodbye and walked away.

"Well," he told the others as he made it back to Avery's truck, "no luck I'm afraid. The plans aren't in the car."

"Right!" Issie said. "Well, now that you've finished keeping us all waiting for nothing, we can finally get going. Let's get these horses loaded, shall we?" She stomped off and grabbed Jasper's lead rope. She was furious! As if it wasn't bad enough that Stuck-up Tucker always wanted Issie's horses, now she was trying to steal Aidan too!

Aidan, meanwhile, couldn't figure out why Issie suddenly seemed to be in such a dark mood with him. As they sat in the horse truck cab together on the way back to Winterflood Farm he finally came out with it and asked her what was wrong.

"What's wrong?" Issie said. "I saw the way Natasha was flirting with you – giggling at everything you said!"

Aidan gave Issie a lopsided grin and pushed his long dark fringe back out of his eyes. "She was flirting with me? Really?"

Issie groaned. "As if you didn't notice!"

"I didn't!" Aidan insisted. "Besides, even if she was flirting with me, I wasn't flirting with her. I would never do that. You know how I feel about you, Issie. You're my girl."

"Am I?" Issie said. She was shaking now, as if all the pent-up emotion and worry that she'd been feeling lately was finally finding its way out of her.

"Issie," said Aidan softly, "what's up? You're not usually like this."

"How would you know what I'm usually like?" Issie said. "Aidan, I hardly ever see you. I mean, I know you've brought the horses here so you can be with me, but you can't stay for ever, can you? I live here in Chevalier Point and you'll go back to Gisborne soon. How are we ever going to see each other then?"

Issie had been hoping at this moment that Aidan would put his arms around her and reassure her that it was all going to be OK. But instead, he went quiet and pushed his hair back out of his eyes to reveal a worried frown.

"I know," he said softly, "you're right. I've been thinking the same thing…" He looked at Issie, his blue eyes full of sorrow. "We need to figure out what we're going to do."

Issie nodded tearfully. "I wish you could just stay in Chevalier Point."

"Me too," Aidan said, "but I can't." He looked ahead at the road, unable to bring himself to look back at Issie's teary eyes. "The gymkhana is next Saturday," he said. "The auction is the weekend after that. I can't stay around any longer. When I sell the horses there's nothing to keep me here any more. After that…" he fought to get the words out, "… after that, I'll be gone. I have to go back to Blackthorn Farm."

CHAPTER 15

As the riders mounted up for the first event of the gymkhana, Stella was in a blind panic. "Has anybody got any hoof oil?" she squeaked. "I forgot mine and Marmite's hooves look terrible!"

"Check in the tack chest in the truck," Kate yelled back at her. She was busy rubbing baby oil over Toby's nose to make his dark muzzle shiny. Issie, meanwhile, was frantically spraying hairspray on a rag and wiping the plaits on Fortune's neck to tidy up any stray hairs.

"OK!" Stella jumped back and gazed at Marmite's shiny hooves with evident satisfaction. "He's done. They look great. Let's go!"

The Best Groomed and Turned-out was the first event of the day and the girls had been working like crazy right up to the very last minute to get their ponies perfectly preened. They lined up nervously in the ring, hoping they hadn't forgotten anything obvious or important as Judge Marjory Allwell surveyed the horses.

Judge Marjory was nervous too. She was still recovering from the dressage day at Chevalier Point when that madman had leapt into the ring and that awful father tried to bribe her! The pony-club committee had to do some sweet-talking to convince her to come back. *Well,* she thought to herself as she walked down the row of riders in their hacking jackets, sitting perfectly still for inspection, *what could possibly go wrong at a gymkhana?*

Judge Marjory stopped in front of a girl on a magnificent chestnut gelding. The horse stood out above all the rest. He was groomed to perfection. Marjory noted that it happened to be the same girl and horse that had won the dressage class that she had judged the last time she was here.

"What is your name, dear?" Judge Marjory asked.

"Natasha Tucker," the girl answered.

"Well, Natasha," Marjory said, "you've done a wonderful job on this horse. Would you mind riding forward a few paces and standing in front of the others so I can get a better look at you?"

Natasha rode Romeo forward and halted square in front of the judge. Marjory Allwell had judged Best Turned-out classes many times and she knew how to thoroughly check over a horse and rider. She looked under the saddle flaps of Natasha's spotless saddle to make sure there was no dirt where the girth buckled up. Then she peered closely at the undersides of Natasha's spit-polished boots to make sure they were clean.

Marjory then worked her way around Romeo, checking on his mane plaits, noting with satisfaction that they were sewn into place with a needle and thread the old-fashioned way, instead of being done quickly with rubber bands. She ran a hand over the gelding's gleaming copper coat to check for dust and admired the slick chequerboard pattern that had been stencilled on to his rump. His tail was the classic show-hack presentation too, plaited neatly at the top, and his hooves were blacked and oiled. There wasn't a single hair out of place on this horse – he was a clear winner here in the senior ring today.

"Your horse is very nicely turned out," Marjory Allwell told Natasha. "What sort of thread did you use to sew these plaits in?"

Natasha looked at her blankly. "I don't know," she said.

Judge Marjory was taken aback. She narrowed her eyes suspiciously. "And what did you use on his hooves?"

"Ummm, I washed them?" said Natasha hopefully.

Marjory Allwell smelt a rat. "Miss Tucker, did you actually sew these plaits?"

"Not exactly…"

The judge raised an eyebrow. "And did you oil and black his hooves?"

"Not really…"

Judge Marjory's face darkened. "Did you do any of the grooming on this horse at all?"

Natasha shook her head. "I keep Romeo stabled with Ginty McLintoch and when I picked him up this morning her grooms had already plaited him for me and done his hooves and the other stuff."

The judge stared at Natasha in stunned disbelief. "Miss Tucker! The rules state quite clearly that you cannot enter the Best Groomed and Turned-out competition unless you have done all the work yourself! I have disqualified girls in the past just because they got their mothers to help them with the plaiting! This is a much more serious situation. By your own admission you have done hardly any work! You have a wonderfully groomed horse, but since it's not your own doing I cannot possibly award you a ribbon."

The scandal spread through the pony club like wildfire. "I think it serves her right," Stella said. "I mean, I put in hours and hours getting Marmite ready. I was up at five this morning plaiting him up!"

"It worked out quite well for us," Kate noted. With Natasha's sudden elimination, Kate and Toby had been bumped up to first place. "Imagine thinking you could enter a horse when you hadn't even done the work yourself!"

Issie shook her head. "I don't think she really meant to cheat – I think she just doesn't realise that other riders have to groom their own horses."

"Oh, come on, Issie!" protested Stella. "She cheated and she got caught. She would be loving it if the same thing happened to you!"

Issie shook her head. "I still feel sorry for her."

"Because she's a cheater?"

"No! I mean I feel sorry for her because of this whole thing with her dad. I'm sure Natasha doesn't even know what he's up to. She thought her dad was actually paying attention to her for once, but in fact, he's just trying to make money off the pony club."

"Has anyone seen Mr Tucker today?" Kate asked.

Issie nodded. "He's over at the judges' marquee. Aidan is keeping an eye on him. He's going to let us know the minute anything happens."

"So at some point today, Mr Tucker is going to meet with the money guys and sign the deal…" Kate said.

"And before he does we still have to somehow get our hands on the blueprints," added Stella.

Issie sighed. "I know. It doesn't sound like much of a plan, does it? But he must have those blueprints with him today. This is our last chance to grab them so we can prove what he's up to."

Over the past week, the girls had failed miserably to come up with a better plan and so far today wasn't going smoothly. Oliver Tucker was already suspicious of Issie. At morning tea time in the judges' marquee he had been talking on his mobile, but as soon as Issie tried to get closer to listen he snapped the phone shut in mid-conversation.

"He knows you're on to him and you're making him twitchy," Aidan pointed out to her. "You stay away from Oliver Tucker. I'll keep an eye on him. Just concentrate on riding Fortune and winning that golden trophy."

All the cups and shields that were up for grabs for today's events were on display on a trestle table in the marquee. The Tucker Trophy eclipsed all the other prizes. It was at least four times the size of any other trophy and the rearing horse looked outrageously glitzy with those turquoise eyes and diamanté mane. Despite the fact that only Chevalier Point riders were eligible to win it, there had been a steady procession of competitors from district pony clubs coming to the tent just to gawp at it, as if it were the *Mona Lisa*.

The scoreboard was set up beside the trophy table, and as the events began to tally up Issie was convinced she was still in with a good chance of winning. After the Best Turned-out drama, Issie had chalked up top points in the first ridden event of the day – Best Rider. Natasha had made a comeback after that in the very next event, winning the Paced & Mannered class. Morgan Chatswood-Smith had won the Open Pony event, with Kate and Toby taking second place, and Natasha had to be satisfied with third.

That brought the morning to a close with the last flat event of the day before lunch break - the Maiden Pony. This was a class for novice horses so only Stella on Marmite and Issie on Fortune were eligible out of the Chevalier Point riders. Competition from the other clubs was stiff, and Stella was beaming from ear to ear when she took first place on Marmite. Issie had come second on Fortune, who had done a lovely figure of eight for the judge and a super rein-back.

There was a huge amount of whooping and clapping from the sidelines as Judge Marjory tied the pretty, gold-trimmed red ribbon around Marmite's neck, and just as much cheering as she put the blue ribbon around Fortune.

"You two have got a fan club, haven't you?" Judge Marjory grinned at the noise from the sidelines. Issie looked up to see her mum and Mrs Tarrant standing beside the arena with Aunt Hester and Araminta Chatswood-Smith.

"Aunty Hess!" Issie was stunned as she rode out of the ring. "Mum didn't tell me you were coming today!"

"That's because I didn't know!" Mrs Brown smiled. "Hester just turned up a moment ago."

"I had to check up on the progress of my ponies, didn't I?" Hester grinned. "Well done, you girls! A few more ribbons around their necks and these ponies will be worth so much more on auction day next weekend!"

Stella's smiled faded as Hester said this. She had really bonded with Marmite over the past two weeks and she had been thrilled when Aidan suggested that she should be the one to ride the brown pony today. After winning at the dressage day, she had leapt at the chance to ride him again. The fact that Marmite was due to be sold at auction in a week's time was not something she wanted to think about.

"When Aidan told me his idea to train the ponies in Chevalier Point," Hester said, "I thought it was just an elaborate plan on his part so that he could hang out with you, Issie. But now that I see how well-schooled these horses have become, I must say he was right to bring them here. Stella did a lovely job riding Marmite in that last event. As for Fortune, he looks like a different pony, doesn't he? What do you think, Araminta?"

"He's a classic Blackthorn," Araminta said, eyeing up the pony's conformation. "Good thick bone, a nice hunter type. But you know me, Hester. I don't care what they look like as long as they can jump."

"I've been showing Araminta a few of my horses," Hester explained to the girls. "Just in case she thinks any of them are suitable to add to her showjumping stable."

"We've already been to Winterflood Farm to check out Strawberry, Roanie and Lulu," Araminta said. "Since it was gymkhana day, we thought this would be the perfect chance to see the other Blackthorns in action."

Despite the fact that Araminta and Hester were only spectators, they were both dressed ready to ride. Aunt Hester was dressed safari-style in khaki jodhpurs and a matching shirt with a leopard-print scarf holding back her curly blonde hair. Araminta was just as chic, in navy jodhpurs with a sky blue blouse and a white and gold Hermes scarf securing her long black ponytail. The two women certainly added a touch of glamour to the pony-club gymkhana.

"Hey, Mum!" Morgan rode up to join them on Black Jack. She hadn't ridden in the last class because Black Jack was too experienced to qualify as a Maiden Pony. "What do you think? I told you that Fortune had potential, didn't I?"

"He certainly does. I'll be looking forward to seeing this pony in the Hunter classes this afternoon," Araminta said to Issie. "Morgan tells me she's seen him jumping at the pony club and he's quite something."

Issie suddenly felt herself swelling up with pride on Fortune's behalf. The kooky little piebald had done so well already today, and if he could just pull off a prize in the Show Hunter competition this afternoon, along with the points they had gathered so far today, Issie knew they had a really good chance of winning the Tucker Trophy.

Her brief moment of pride was short-lived, however, because on the way back to the horse truck, she was jolted back to reality. In the showjumping ring the men were now beginning to erect the course. Her heart plummeted as she looked at the jumps circuit.

It was a classic, simple Show Hunter course. There were three white gates, a brush fence and then another gate around the sides of the arena. They all looked fine, but the fence in the middle of the ring gave Issie a sick feeling. They were putting in a full wire fence! It was just like the one she had fallen at during the training with Avery.

Issie felt the butterflies churning up already. She had been hoping against the odds that there wouldn't be a wire to jump in the course today.

"Issie?" Stella came riding up next to her. "Kate and I are going to get some crisps at the clubroom on the way back to the truck – you want to come?"

Issie shook her head. "You go on without me – I'll meet you guys later. I've got to go and do something."

Issie realised now that she had to find Avery. She needed her instructor's help to resolve Fortune's problems with the wire or she would never get a clear round. If she couldn't make it over that fence, she didn't stand a chance of winning the Show Hunter and her hopes of taking home the Tucker Trophy were doomed.

CHAPTER 16

Avery was having issues of his own when Issie found him at the judges' marquee.

"What's up?" he said. "Can it wait? I'm in a bit of a flap trying to get these flag race entries sorted…"

"Not really," Issie said. "Please, Tom, I need your help."

Avery put down the box of entry forms and turned to her. "What's the problem?"

"You know how Fortune and I had that fall when we were training over the wire fence?" Issie asked.

"I remember," he said, "but you got back on and you aced it."

"That's the thing," Issie said. "I managed to get Fortune over it then, but I could tell that he was really frightened and there's no way he'll jump it again." She felt like she was about to burst into tears. "And now there's one in the Show Hunter class and if I can't somehow get him over it, then there's no way we can get a clear round and win it and…"

"Hey, hey, Issie, calm down," Avery said gently. "You're getting yourself all worked up."

Issie wiped the tears from her eyes and took a deep breath.

"Feeling better?"

"Uh-huh," said Issie shakily.

"Listen," Avery said, "this is no big deal. We just need to get your confidence back."

Issie frowned. "My confidence?" She was confused. "But it's Fortune. He's the one who's scared. He's totally spooked by the wire!"

"Really?" Avery said. "Are you sure that's what's happening, Issie?"

"What do you mean?"

"A horse can sense when his rider isn't totally committed to jumping a fence," said Avery. "The day that you and Fortune had your fall, you were tensed up and your body language was all wrong as you approached the jump. You weren't riding positively and instead, you rode as if you were braced for Fortune to refuse."

"You're saying it was my fault?" Issie couldn't believe it.

Avery shook his head. "I'm not saying you did it on purpose. But the mind controls the body. I think there was part of you that didn't believe that Fortune would jump and so instinctively, you held yourself back and rode defensively as if you were prepared to stop."

Even though Issie didn't want to admit it, she knew that Avery was right. She had been riding totally differently when she'd tried to jump the wire. She never expected Fortune to jump – and that was why she'd failed.

"It is me," she said quietly. "I'm the one who's causing the problem."

Avery nodded. "It's important that you can admit it. And it's more common than you think. Every rider in the world faces a bogey fence at some time, Issie."

"So it's really all my fault?" Issie asked tearfully.

"Not entirely. The problem is, once a horse starts baulking, it becomes a vicious circle," Avery confirmed. "Once you feel that fear and indecision, you pass it on to your horse. Fortune has sensed your lack of faith in him and it's made him confused. You ride him at the jump, but you don't really believe he's going to take it and so he stops."

Issie groaned. "So now it's impossible to solve?"

"I never said that." Avery shook his head. "I'm sure we can get you and Fortune jumping the wire with no trouble."

Avery reached up and took Fortune's reins. "Hop off," he said.

Issie was confused. "What?"

"You heard me," Avery said. "Hop off."

"But why?"

Avery smiled. "Because I'm going to ride Fortune."

Avery led Fortune over to the warm-up area and explained his theory to Issie as they walked side by side. "This horse is not afraid of the wire. Once you see for yourself that he can jump it, then you'll have faith in him and you'll be able to commit completely to the fence."

He turned to her. "Now give me a leg-up, will you?"

Issie had seen Avery ride, but he had never been on one of her horses before – and he had never ridden here at the pony club. He looked so strange sitting up there on Fortune – and his appearance wasn't helped by the fact that his long, lanky legs made him much too large for the piebald pony.

"I'll just settle him in," Avery told her. "And then I'll pop him over the wire a couple of times."

Avery gathered up the reins and rode Fortune off at a brisk trot, working him around the arena. The first thing that Issie noticed was how nicely Fortune moved with Tom riding him. His trot was alert and collected as Avery got him on the bit. Fortune arched his neck and used his hindquarters beautifully. Issie watched in amazement as Avery made every move that she tried to do seem totally effortless.

Issie was reminded of just what a great rider Avery must once have been. Her instructor had ridden at the Olympics and the Badminton Horse Trials. It might have been a long time ago now, but Avery still handled a horse better than anyone else she knew.

There were three warm-up jumps set up today, including a wire fence, and several riders were using them now that the Show Hunter class was about to get under way. Avery rode respectfully, as professional riders do, making sure that he didn't get in the way as another rider was about to jump. Then he took his turn, coming in at a trot to face the wire fence. Taking it at a trot! Issie couldn't believe it. But Avery knew what he was doing. He let Fortune put in two easy canter strides just before the jump and the piebald popped over it as if it weren't even there!

Avery gave Fortune a slappy pat on his broad black and white neck as they hit the ground on the other side and then he immediately came around once more to take the fence again. This time he cantered Fortune in all the way at a steady pace and once again Fortune leapt the wire with total ease.

Avery cantered around and did a loop, coming in from the other side of the fence this time. Issie watched the piebald arc neatly over with his ears pricked forward. Avery had been totally right. Fortune wasn't scared of the wire. It had been Issie's problem all along.

As Avery came trotting back over to her Issie felt embarrassed.

Avery smiled at her. "If anything, it's my fault. I should have made sure that you got your confidence back after you fell. I didn't realise what you were going through. I guess I think of you as bulletproof, Issie. But even really good riders can have their nerve tested and I should have picked up on the warning signs."

He vaulted down off Fortune's back. "Anyway, do you believe in your horse now?"

Issie nodded. "I do."

Avery smiled again. "Then I think it's time you got back on and gave it a go yourself." He looked at his watch. "They're about to get under way with the afternoon jumping. It'll be time for you to go into the ring soon."

Issie put on her helmet then Avery gave her a leg-up and she shortened her stirrups, adjusting their length back to her jumping height. She was just getting settled into the saddle when Stella suddenly cantered into the practice ring, waving frantically at them.

"What's going on?" Stella said. "Why are you still here? Why aren't you in the Show Hunter ring?"

"What are you talking about?" asked Issie.

"The Show Hunter class has started!" Stella said. "You're supposed to be the second rider to go! They've already called your name twice."

Issie felt as if iced water had suddenly been poured into her veins. She had never expected the Hunter Class to begin so quickly after lunch break! She hadn't even had time to try a practice jump and if she didn't get into the arena fast, she might not even get the chance to compete.

"Go now!" Stella yelled. "They'll call you once more and then you'll be eliminated. GO!"

Issie reached the arena just in time to hear her name being called over the loudspeaker. She was about to ride into the ring when she felt a hand clasp her arm. It was Aidan!

"He's on the move!" Aidan said.

"Who?" Issie didn't know what Aidan was talking about.

"Mr Tucker," Aidan said. "I've been tailing him all morning and he must have realised because just a moment ago he managed to lose me and then he totally disappeared. He's gone, Issie! I can't find him anywhere on the club grounds. I think whatever he has planned is about to happen!"

Issie looked around, panic-struck. Oliver Tucker was nowhere in sight. And she was due in the ring pronto!

"I've got to go in right now or I'll be eliminated," she told Aidan. "Keep an eye out for Mr Tucker. I won't be long. I'll talk to you in a minute, OK?"

Aidan reluctantly let go of her arm and Issie rode straight into the ring and saluted the judge. She acknowledged Issie's arrival with a return salute and Issie urged Fortune into a canter, doing a big circle to get the horse into a steady stride before facing up to the first jump.

She had never felt more unprepared in a show ring than she did at that moment. She hadn't even had a chance to do any of the jumps, let alone practise over the wire. And then Aidan grabbing her like that just as she was about to enter the ring!

Issie could feel her heart pounding in her chest. She had to calm down and focus. Avery was right. She had to keep it together if she expected Fortune to make it a clear round. And she had to go clear if she wanted to win the golden trophy.

Issie rode hard at the first fence, picking up Fortune's stride, pressing him into a strong canter. The piebald jumped the white gate easily with perfect Show Hunter style. He took the second and third gates just as smoothly and did a U-turn at the far end of the ring, looping round to canter back over the final fences. Ahead of them was the brush fence, the last white gate and then finally, they would need to circle into the middle of the ring to jump the wire. Issie felt a surge of excitement as Fortune pulled against her hands, keen to get to the next jump. The piebald was clearly loving it and Issie was ready to go with him.

She steadied Fortune and looked over the next fence: the brush. From this angle she could see back across the pony-club field and on to the golf course. Ahead of her, out on the green, was a sight she hadn't expected to see. Oliver Tucker was driving a golf buggy like a man possessed, across the fairway towards the furthest end of the course. Beside him, on the passenger seat, Issie could see a long plastic tube. The blueprints! He must be on his way to the meeting with his backers!

Issie looked around frantically. Aidan hadn't spotted Mr Tucker yet. And Stella and Kate were both over at the practice arena warming up. By the time Issie finished her round and raised the alarm it would be too late.

Issie had to make a choice. If she wanted to stop Mr Tucker, she needed to act now. The golden trophy with its turquoise eyes and sparkly ruby hooves flashed through her mind. She imagined going up in front of everyone at prize-giving to accept the trophy, and the look on Natasha's face as she took it from under her nose. Then she let the dream go. The pony club was more important than any prize.

"Come on, Fortune!" She turned the pony hard, tugging on the right rein to turn him away from the brush. Fortune had the jump in his sights and was confused as they galloped straight past it. But he didn't fight Issie as she rode him straight towards the fenceline.

On the sidelines the spectators had noticed that something was wrong with the competitor in the ring. Why wasn't she taking on any of the jumps? And where on earth was she going?

Avery, Mrs Brown, Araminta and Aunty Hester were all completely bewildered as they stood and watched Issie's bizarre turn.

"What the heck is going on?" Hester said. "Is Fortune bolting?"

Avery shook his head. "It's not the horse, it's Issie. She's riding him at the back fence!"

Between the golf club and the pony club was a full wire fence, a little higher than the one Issie had been going to jump for the Show Hunter.

As Issie approached the fence she felt a brief moment of nerves – a tightening in her belly. This was a real fence, not a show ring jump. She couldn't afford to make a mistake.

She tried to remember what Avery had said about believing that she could do it. She tried to positively visualise herself soaring over the wire, landing safely on the other side. "Go on, go on, GO ON!" Issie was talking to herself and didn't realise that her whisper was becoming a shout as she came in for the last stride at the wire. In that crucial moment, she knew the truth. If she didn't have total faith, she would fail, Fortune would baulk and all would be lost, including the pony club. Issie held her breath. And jumped.

CHAPTER 17

Fortune took the full wire fence like a true Show Hunter, never breaking stride as he hit the ground and continued straight on across the flat, manicured expanse of the golf course.

Issie pressed the piebald on into a gallop, cutting through the middle of the eighteenth hole, ignoring the shouts of horror from the golfers who were aghast at the sight of a horse churning up their precious grass. Fortune's hooves pounded into the carpet of perfect green lawn, flinging up great divots of turf.

On the other side of the wire fence, back at the pony club, the Show Hunter class was in chaos. Could this really be happening? Had one of Chevalier Point's club members just taken off in the middle of her round and jumped the fence into the golf course?

Avery had been watching in amazement as Issie and the piebald suddenly veered completely off course and jumped the golf-club fence. "Has she gone totally mad?" he said to Araminta and Hester. "What the blazes is she up to?"

They didn't have a chance to answer because there was a beep-beep sound and Aidan careered up on the far side of the fence driving a golf cart.

"I saw everything. She's after Mr Tucker!" Aidan shouted. "He's taken off in a golf cart. He must be going to the meeting!"

Avery looked at Aidan. "What are you talking about? What meeting? Has the whole world gone mad? Why are you driving a golf cart?"

"I borrowed it off some golfers who weren't looking," Aidan grinned.

"You mean you stole it!" Avery was completely beside himself now.

"Yeah, but I needed to," said Aidan. "We need to catch up to Issie. She's in danger!"

"She's in danger of me wringing her neck for doing this," Avery said. "Now do you want to explain what on earth is going on here?"

Aidan shook his head. "No time. Jump in and I'll tell you on the way."

By the time Avery had vaulted the fence and joined Aidan in the golf cart, Issie was already halfway along the fairway, galloping hard across the immaculately kept grass, closing in on Oliver Tucker.

Natasha's dad was driving as fast as he could, but the golf cart could only handle certain terrain. He couldn't speed along the hills and bumps, or through the long grass and bunkers, so he stuck to the fairways, zipping along over the manicured grass. This was where Issie had the advantage – she could take short cuts. As Oliver Tucker scooted on ahead she swerved to the right, riding down into the hollow pit of a sand bunker and up the other side. As she rose back up out, she was alarmed to see a group of golfers standing right in her path.

"Out of my way, please!" she shouted at the group of men carrying golf bags and clubs. "Coming through!"

The last thing the golfers expected to see on a lovely afternoon on the golf course was a girl on a horse about to mow them down. One of them actually shrieked, and all four of them dropped their clubs and scattered to get out of her way.

"Sorry!' Issie yelled as she rode through them. "It's an emergency!"

"What are you playing at? Get that bloomin' beast off the golf course!" one of the men screamed after her. "I'm reporting you! This is an outrage!"

All over the course, golfers were whipping out their mobile phones to dial the clubhouse. Issie knew it was only a matter of minutes before they alerted Gordon Cheeseman, but she couldn't afford to worry about him. Right now all she cared about was catching up with Oliver Tucker before it was too late.

Ahead of her the golf cart was in her sights. He must have had the pedal to the floor because it was going like a bat out of hell. She had no idea those things could go so fast! Oliver Tucker was scooting over the fairways and in the distance, Issie could see a group of men dressed in suits, some of them holding briefcases and talking on their mobiles as they waited for him. They must be the financial backers! She had to get to Oliver Tucker before he met with them and they exchanged contracts and the plans.

"C'mon, Fortune!" Issie let the reins inch through her fingers and she urged the piebald on with her legs. "We need to move it!"

Fortune wasn't particularly built for speed. He was a Blackthorn Pony, robust and stocky, with a conformation made for jumping. But the past months of solid training that Issie had done with the piebald had made him fit and lean, and he was able to keep striding out without tiring. As Issie asked him to go faster Fortune genuinely did his best for the girl. He trusted his rider because he knew now that she had faith in him. It was her confidence in Fortune that had made him soar over the wire only a few moments ago.

As they raced after the golf cart Fortune gave it everything he had, straining and stretching his muscles as his strides flattened out, his gallop chewing up the grass beneath him. They were gaining on the golf cart now, catching up fast. Oliver Tucker had his foot down, but it wasn't enough. Fortune was faster, and they would reach him before he made it to the men at the end of the course.

Oliver Tucker looked back over his shoulder. He could see that the girl on the piebald was close now, and it was obvious that she knew too much. How did he get himself into this mess? The plans for his luxury apartments were on the seat beside him and the contracts too. The deal was nearly done. He wasn't about to quit!

Oliver Tucker looked at the golf bag in the passenger seat. Maybe he wouldn't have to give up – not just yet. This girl had bitten off more than she could chew, and now she was going to pay the price!

Still driving with his right hand, Oliver Tucker used his other hand to reach into the golf bag and grab a fistful of hard, white balls. He pivoted around in his seat as the girl got close to him and took aim, hurling a ball straight at her.

Behind the golf car, Issie saw the ball coming just in time and managed somehow to duck her head so that it missed her by a whisker. She had only just looked back up again when a second ball flew at her and then another and another! The fourth ball hit Fortune on the chest and the piebald startled, swerving to one side. Issie let out a squeal, but she managed to stay on and keep galloping.

Issie was getting closer now and Oliver Tucker was rummaging around in the bag again for more ammunition. He grabbed another handful of balls and pivoted around in his seat to face her. He took aim, and was about to fire one straight at her, when he heard something on the course ahead of him that made him stop and spin back around.

The sound was the thunder of hoofbeats. There was another horse on the golf course, right in Oliver Tucker's path, heading straight on a collision course with the golf cart.

Oliver Tucker dropped the golf balls and grabbed the steering wheel in desperation. The grey pony in front of him had no rider, so why was it galloping straight at him? Oliver Tucker honked his horn, but the grey pony didn't falter. It was still coming for him!

Oliver Tucker steeled himself. If this horse wanted to play chicken and wait to see who would lose their nerve and swerve first then it was going to lose! As Mystic bore down on the golf cart Oliver Tucker put his foot to the floor. He kept driving straight at the pony, daring the dapple-grey to keep coming.

They were just metres away from each other when Oliver Tucker realised the awful truth. The pony wasn't going to get out of the way. Mystic was not about to give up. He was willing to crash straight into the golf cart if that was what it took to stop this man. In a blind panic, Oliver Tucker grabbed the golf cart's steering wheel and screwed a hard ninety-degree turn, spinning the cart to the right to get out of the pony's path.

The manoeuvre didn't go well at all. Oliver Tucker

had forgotten that he wasn't driving a Ferrari. He was only in a golf cart and they don't have the power or precision of a flash sports car. As he spun the wheel with his foot down hard on the accelerator the golf cart went totally out of control and skidded across the golf green like a hockey puck sliding across ice, bouncing over the fairway and flinging him about like a rag doll.

Oliver Tucker had no choice but to hang on for dear life as the cart hit the edge of a bunker with a dramatic bounce, flew up into the air and came down on the slope on the other side that led to the water trap. He was flung forward by the impact and the engine kept gunning as the cart skidded down the bank towards the water. With his foot stuck on the pedal, the engine was still revving as the golf cart struck the pond. It hit the water and kept on going, submerging deeper and deeper as it puttered out to the middle of the pond, until only the roof, the top of the bonnet and seats were above the surface.

When Issie arrived at the edge of the pond on Fortune moments later, Oliver Tucker was clambering out frantically, trying to escape the water which was seeping over the seats of the cart. Like a cat trying to keep its paws dry, he was struggling to keep his flashy designer suit from getting wet. He scrambled out to the bonnet and then pulled himself on to the roof of the cart as it sank deeper into the mud of the pond.

In his haste, Oliver Tucker had left the document tube on the seat of the cart. But it hadn't sunk because it was made of sealed plastic. As the golf cart seats disappeared under the water it had floated merrily away. Issie could see the cylinder bobbing about in the middle of the pond.

"C'mon, Fortune!" She clucked the piebald up to the edge of the pond and he walked into the water without hesitation. As Oliver Tucker watched from his refuge on the roof of the golf cart Issie and Fortune ploughed into the pond. Issie steered Fortune with one hand and scooped up the document tube with the other, before turning the piebald around and heading back towards the grassy bank.

"What are you doing?" Oliver Tucker said as she rode past him. "Those blueprints are mine. Hey! Come back and get me off this thing! The blasted cart is sinking! This pond's got eels in it. Filthy creatures! I can't get this suit wet – it cost a fortune! Come back here! Do you hear me!"

On the hill overlooking the pond, Mr Tucker's financial backers had heard him. They had witnessed the whole spectacle of the golf-cart chase. Now they were piling into their own golf carts and swiftly leaving the scene. They didn't have any intention of wading in to help the property developer either. The men in suits had all taken one look at the unfolding drama and wisely decided that Oliver Tucker was not the most reputable man to be in business with after all, and they weren't going to hang around any longer.

Issie had just reached dry land again when there was a honk behind her and she turned to see Avery and Aidan in their golf cart zipping across the grass towards her.

"Issie!" Aidan called out. "Are you all right?"

"I'm fine," said Issie. She gestured towards the pond. "I think Mr Tucker could do with some help though."

Avery grinned at the sight of the businessman stuck on the roof of the golf cart. "Everything all right, Ollie?" he asked sarcastically.

"Get me off this cart now, Avery, or there'll be hell to pay!" Oliver Tucker shouted back in reply.

Issie passed the plastic tube containing the blueprints to Avery. "He'll be the one who's in trouble when the pony-club committee sees this."

"What's in here?" Avery asked.

Issie smiled. "Something much more important than a golden trophy."

CHAPTER 18

When Gordon Cheeseman arrived at the scene a few moments later Avery allowed the puce-faced golf-club manager to have his rant about the outrage of horses on his golf course. He listened to an endless stream of threats and accusations and finally, when Gordon was showing no sign of running out of steam, Avery decided he'd heard enough.

"You can stop yelling and start listening," Avery told him, "because as far as I can see, Gordon, you're in this up to your neck. Making secret deals with Oliver Tucker to force the pony club off our land so that he could set up a luxury country-club complex? I'm sure the district council will be very interested to know the details and see the papers in here that you've signed along with the blueprints!"

"You can't do that!" Gordon Cheeseman sputtered.

"Never mind him!" Oliver Tucker shouted from the roof of the golf cart. "Get me off here now, Gordon, or our deal's off! I have to catch up with my investors."

"Oliver," Gordon Cheeseman said, "the tow truck is coming. I'm going to call the police too. When they hear about how the pony club vandalised my golf course today this will just add more weight to our case..."

"No!" Oliver Tucker shouted. "No police!"

"Oh, for God's sake, Gordon!" Avery snapped. "You still don't get it, do you? Tucker doesn't want you to call the cops because he's the one who's been causing you all the trouble! He was sabotaging your club and trying to pin it on my riders so that he could convince you to sign on the dotted line. He's behind ALL of it."

"Oliver?" Gordon Cheeseman's eyes widened beneath his tam-o'-shanter as he realised for the first time just how badly he'd been duped. "Is this true?"

Oliver Tucker groaned and slumped down on the roof of the golf cart with his head in his hands. "Go back to your clubhouse, Gordon," he said without looking up. "You're an idiot."

"But what about my golf course?" huffed Gordon

Cheeseman. He turned to Issie. "Your horses have ruined it. You'll have to pay for the repairs."

Avery shook his head. "Issie isn't paying a jot, Gordon. If anything, you should be grateful to this girl for exposing Tucker for the fraud he really is – even if she had to chase him over your golf course to do it."

He paused. "Of course, if you'd still like to involve the police, we'd be happy to call them. I'm sure they'd be more concerned by your backroom deals than they would be by a few hoof prints on a golf course."

Gordon Cheeseman glared angrily at Avery. He could see that if he pushed his luck, he would end up in more trouble than it was worth.

"All right!" he snarled. "Get both your horses off my green immediately, Avery. Let's all forget any of this ever happened, shall we?" There was bitter resignation in his voice.

Horses? As far as Avery and Aidan knew there had only ever been one horse on the golf course – Fortune. They hadn't seen Mystic confronting Oliver Tucker's golf cart. And now that the danger was over, Mystic was gone. Issie looked around, but she could see no sign of the grey pony who had turned up just in time to save her once again.

There were people all over the golf course now. The golfers had given up on their games and come to watch the spectacle as the tow truck turned up to hoist the golf cart and a distraught Oliver Tucker out of the water.

"I guess we should head back to the pony club. Everyone will be wondering what's happened to us after your dramatic exit from the Show Hunter ring," said Avery.

Issie grinned. "He jumped that wire beautifully, didn't he?"

"I guess he did," Avery agreed. "Clearly, it's not a bogey fence for you any more then?"

Issie shook her head. "Fortune favours the brave!"

Aidan patted the piebald on his sweaty neck. "Good boy, Fortune." He smiled at Issie. "Do you want me to ride him home? You can go in the golf cart with Avery if you like. You must be pretty shaken up."

"Are you kidding?" Issie grinned. "I've always wanted to ride on the golf course. It's so beautiful here with all that perfect grass and the trees. Can you imagine how cool it would be to build some cross-country jumps on it?"

Avery smiled. "I think hell would freeze over before Gordon Cheeseman agreed to that."

Issie's grin grew more wicked. "I'd love one more gallop at least. Do you think Mr Cheeseman would stop me if I galloped Fortune back home again?"

"He'd have to catch you first," Avery smiled back. "Go on! Off you go!"

Oliver Tucker was absent that afternoon as an emergency meeting of the pony-club committee was held in the Chevalier Point clubroom. Avery stood at the podium with the blueprints for Oliver Tucker's luxury country-club apartments in his hands and explained to the committee how the property developer had devised the plan to move the pony club to the River Paddock so he could take the land. The committee listened carefully and made a unanimous decision. For the first time ever in the history of Chevalier Point Pony Club, the president was impeached. Oliver Tucker had abused the trust of the club and was fired from his presidency on the spot.

With all the members still gathered in the clubroom, everyone decided that this was a good time to hold the prize-giving. "This is going to be good!" Stella said as she grabbed a seat next to Issie. "I can't wait!"

"Why?" Issie was puzzled.

"Oh, that's right," Stella grinned. "You missed everything. You were too busy chasing golf carts when all the action was happening."

"What action?" asked Issie. "What are you talking about?"

"The Tucker Trophy!" Stella said. "You'll see in a minute... just watch!"

Due to Mr Tucker's expulsion, former club president Mrs Tarrant was asked up on to the stage to present the Tucker Trophy.

"The first year of this new prize for the club's senior riders was a closely fought contest," she announced. "The points were tight, but in the final tally, one rider managed to score consistently more with a great final round in the Show Hunter event."

Mrs Tarrant smiled. "Would Kate Knight please come up and receive her award as the winner of the Natasha Tucker Memorial Trophy!"

"Ohmygod!" Issie shrieked. "You're kidding me! Kate won it?"

Kate had been thrilled to bits when she took the first place in the Show Hunter class, but hadn't even considered her points tally until she saw the scoreboard moments ago when they came into the clubroom. It was still sinking in that she had won, and as she stepped up to accept her prize she looked completely stunned.

She was laughing a minute later when she realised she could barely carry it by herself. "I'm going to have to load it into the horse truck to get it home!" she giggled as she set it down in the corner of the clubroom. The girls were admiring Kate's prize when a hand reached out and tapped Kate on the shoulder.

"I just wanted to say congratulations," Natasha Tucker said.

Natasha looked a mess. She had clearly been crying, but Issie figured this had more to do with the revelations about her dad than it had to do with losing the trophy to Kate.

In the final Show Hunter contest the pressure had proved too much for Natasha. She had lost her cool and overcooked Romeo. As a result, the Selle Francais had put in a shocking round, baulking three times and being eliminated. Naturally, being Natasha, she had blamed her horse for her failure. Romeo was already on the truck on his way back to Ginty McLintoch's stables with a 'For Sale' sticker on him.

Natasha stuck out her hand. "You did really well to win it," she said. Then as Kate shook hands with her she added, "But don't get used to it. I plan to win it back next year."

Stella watched with awe as Natasha marched out of the door. "She's unstoppable."

"I'm not so sure," said Issie. "She must be pretty upset about her dad. Maybe this is her warped way of trying to be friends again."

"Yeah, well, funny way of going about it!" Stella scoffed.

Losing the Tucker Trophy to one of her best friends made Issie even happier about her decision to leap the fence in the middle of the Show Hunter class. As far as she was concerned Fortune might not have got a ribbon for it, but the way he took the full wire fence was a sign of his true greatness.

It turned out she wasn't the only one who thought so. As she was unplaiting his mane and getting ready to bandage him up for the trip home in the truck Aunt Hester suddenly appeared with Araminta at her side.

"Don't bother with the bandages," Hester said. "Fortune isn't going back to Winterflood Farm."

"Why not?" Issie asked.

"He's not being auctioned any more," Hester said, "because I've just sold him."

Issie couldn't believe it. "Who to?"

"Me!" Araminta smiled. "I've just given your aunt a sizeable cheque for this corker of a pony!"

"I was quite keen on Fortune when I saw you riding him earlier today, but what really got me was the way he took that fence and jumped on to the golf course!"

Issie was amazed. Araminta ran one of the best jumping stables in the country – and she had just paid top dollar for Fortune!

"He's got such courage, hasn't he?" Araminta enthused. "And a really scopey jump. It's early days of course, but I really think he may turn out to be one of my best horses!"

"You wouldn't have thought that if you'd seen him two months ago!" Issie laughed. Then she realised how awful that must have sounded. "Sorry, Aunty Hess!"

"Don't be silly," Hester said. "You're quite right, Issie. You've done wonders schooling Fortune into a quality showjumping prospect. You should be very proud of him."

"I am," Issie said, stroking the piebald's velvety nose. "I really am."

Then turning back to her aunt she said, "So there's just

five horses left for the auction next weekend?"

"Four actually," Hester smiled. "I sold another one today."

At that moment, Stella raced around the corner of the horse truck with a huge smile on her face. "Has Hester told you the news?" she asked Issie. "Mum has agreed to buy Marmite for me!"

Another Blackthorn Pony had found a home and Stella, finally, had found herself a new ride. As for the four others: "Aidan will stay here for the rest of the week sorting them out for auction," Hester told Issie. "After that I really can't do without him at the farm any longer."

Hester was right of course. Aidan needed to go home to Blackthorn Farm. But what did that mean for Issie? After their heart-to-heart the other day, she was convinced that Aidan thought it was too hard to keep their relationship going. It was clear that he wanted them to split up. He just didn't know how to tell her. Well, she would make it easy on him. She was going to be brave and break up with him instead.

"You're a twit."

It wasn't the response Issie had been expecting. Her jaw hung open in shock as Aidan grinned at her from ear to ear.

"What?"

"I said you're a twit!" Aidan smiled. "Of course I don't want to split up with you!"

"Well, it's just that you seemed really unhappy about never spending time together and now you'll be going back to Blackthorn Farm again soon and I know how hard it is being apart and…"

"Issie, I am unhappy about going home!" Aidan said. "I'm miserable about being away from you, but that doesn't mean that splitting up is the answer."

He looked at her with those startling blue eyes and took her hand. "Issie, when I saw you take off over the golf course after Oliver Tucker I was so worried. I couldn't stand it if anything happened to you."

"Aidan!" Issie smiled. "Nothing is going to happen to me!"

"I know that," Aidan said. "I know you can take care of yourself. That's one of the things I love about you most. Watching you ride today made me realise how I really feel, and how special you are.

"It doesn't matter how much distance there is between us. You're my girl, Issie. So what if I have to drive for six hours just to take you to the movies now and then? We will make it work somehow. I can come and visit you on weekends and you can come and stay at the farm sometimes. After all, it's not like we're living in different countries or anything."

Issie grinned. "Yeah, I guess not. You're right. I was being a drama queen."

"So we're good then?"

"We're better than good!" Issie smiled back.

Aidan put his arms around her and Issie shut her eyes as she felt his cheek pressing against her own and his lips...

"Hey! You two! Stop the smoochy stuff!" It was Stella.

"What do you want, Stella?" Aidan groaned.

"I don't want anything," Stella said. "It's Avery. He's called a special meeting of club members right now. Come on!"

In the clubroom, the other riders has already assembled and sat down on the old, overstuffed armchairs and folding chairs. At the front of the room, Avery was back at the podium and this time he had three other people with him. One of them Issie recognised as the judge from their class today, Marjory Allwell.

"I thought I should do this while everyone was still here since we don't have another rally for two weeks," Avery explained. "You'll recognise the judges from today's gymkhana. I would like to thank Judges Marjory Allwell,

Angela Funkel and Barbara McLean. They've had quite a wild time here today at Chevalier Point!"

The club members gave a round of applause and then Avery continued. "As well as judging your classes today these ladies are also working on another very special task, acting as the selection panel to choose the National Young Rider squad."

Issie, Stella and Kate all looked at each other as Avery continued. "I am incredibly proud to announce today that four of those riders will be from the Chevalier Point Pony Club!"

There was wild applause at this news and then Avery spoke again. "I'd like to thank our selection panel for their choices. Would the following riders please step forward when I call your names."

There was silence in the clubroom. You could have cut the air with a knife.

"Morgan Chatswood-Smith, please come up here!" Avery said. Morgan looked totally surprised as she stepped up to stand beside Chevalier Point's head instructor.

"And today's Tucker Trophy winner, Kate Knight, please?" Avery called out. Kate, who was still recovering from receiving the golden trophy, nearly fell off her chair. "The third name on my list is... Stella Tarrant," Avery grinned. There was whooping from the crowd as Stella blushed bright red with delight at having made the squad.

"And last, but not least, our golf-course crusader, Isadora Brown!" said Avery.

Issie couldn't believe it! She had made the squad and her two best friends and Morgan were in too!

As she made her way to the podium Issie had never been more thrilled.

"Congratulations to those who've made the squad," said Avery. "In just one month, we'll be flying to take up the Young Rider Challenge in Melbourne, Australia!"

She was going to Australia? Ohmygod! Issie looked for Aidan's face in the crowd, her heart racing as she recalled his words. *It's not like we're living in different countries or anything.*

She saw Aidan's heartbroken blue eyes staring back at her and realised that once again her world had been turned upside down.

She was going to represent her country riding against the most talented young riders in Australia! It was one of the best moments of her life, and as she shook Marjory Allwell's hand she tried hard to smile. Only Aidan, standing in the back row, saw the tears in her eyes.